CHECKMATE

THE HARRY STARKE NOVELS BOOK 4

BLAIR HOWARD

CHECKMATE

A Harry Starke Novel

ISBN-13: 978-1523729814

ISBN-10: 1523729813

1

"So, that's ten dollars you owe me," he said as he plucked his ball from the sixth green's hole.

"Yeah, Dad. I know. I can count," I said. "You birdied the third hole and this one." I looked at the other two members of our foursome, Judge Henry Strange and ADA Lawrence "Larry" Spruce. They were both grinning at me. They knew my father well.

How the hell he gets anyone to play with him, I have no clue. He's a shark. He reluctantly admits to a five handicap, but often plays scratch golf. In another life he probably could have turned pro. He has a caustic sense of humor, loves to play mind games, and gives not an inch. Even so, I love to play with him.

August Stark, my father, is something of a celebrity and so, I suppose, am I, having become one only lately, and not by choice. He's a lawyer, and a very successful one, with an estimated net worth of close to $200 million. With silver hair and moustache, he cuts an imposing figure even at sixty-six. He's a big man, an inch taller than me, and since he works out every other morning he's sick-eningly healthy, and carries not a pound of extra fat. He's also the most competitive man I've ever met, both in the courtroom and on the golf course. He takes more delight in winning ten bucks on the greens than he does in winning a multi-million-dollar class action.

It was Thursday morning, a little after nine o'clock, and the judge and I were playing him and Larry Spruce. The stakes were a whopping twenty-five dollars on the game, with five-dollar birdies. So now I owed the old man an extra ten, and he was needling me about it, and it was working. It always did.

We moved to the next tee. Having birdied the last hole, the Old Man – he hates to be called that - had the honor, which meant he was first to play. The seventh, a dead-straight par five, stretched away some 558 yards to an elevated, postage-stamp-sized green. The fairway was narrow, with a forced carry off the tee of some 120 yards, and bounded by heavy rough on both sides and a river off to the right. It was a daunting hole that demanded an accurate drive to a less than generous landing area, a long straight second, and an even more accurate approach shot. A hook off the tee would put me in the rough to the right, if not the river; a slice, and I'd spend the rest of the day looking for my ball in knee-high grass.

The foursome in front of us was almost at the green, so we were clear to go.

For me, with an iffy nine handicap, the seventh was always a safe three iron off the tee. For my old man.... Well, I watched as he dragged the big dog out of his bag and proceeded to hammer the ball 290 yards straight down the center of the fairway, leaving himself with an easy five iron and a wedge into the green. He watched it settle onto the short grass, then turned and gifted me with one of his triumphant grins. *Oh my God. Give me a break, please.*

Larry, not a little intimidated by his partner's stunning shot, stood looking down at the three clubs he'd carried from the cart to the tee. He shook his head, grabbed his three iron, hit it fat, and barely cleared the forced carry. He'd just turned a tough par five into an even tougher par six.

I set the ball low on the tee, and addressed it with my three iron. On a good day I could hit the club 200, maybe 210 yards. Today, with the Old Man leaning casually on his driver, smiling, watching... well, you get the idea.

"Now, son. No guts, no birdies. Be a man. Put that thing back in the bag and hit the ball with a proper club."

"Screw you, Dad. Play your mind games on somebody else." I swung, nailed it right on the sweet spot, and watched the ball start out low then gather altitude as the spin lifted it over the carry and on down the fairway a good 225 yards, leaving me with a solid five iron and then an eight iron to the flag—so I hoped. It was one of my best shots, but not quite good enough.

Judge Strange was teeing his ball when we heard a shout.

"Hey Harry! Over here!" It was Greg Holloway. He was standing by his cart on the right side of the seventh green, in the rough close to the river's edge, waving both arms over his head. I figured he must have put his ball in the water. I waved back, then turned to watch the judge make his shot.

"Harry! Harry Starke!"

What the hell? I turned again. He was still waving his arms.

"C'mere, Harry. Now. We've got a body in the water!"

I turned to the others. "Did he say 'body?'"

"I think he did, "August said. "Better go take a look, Harry."

We ran to the carts, threw our clubs into the bags, and raced off down the fairway toward the still-waving Greg Holloway.

"Over there." He pointed as he ran toward the water's edge.

"Hey. Whoa," I yelled. "Don't go down there, Greg. Stay away. Don't disturb anything."

The woman was just a few feet from the riverbank, lying on her back in six inches of water. She looked peaceful, but there was no doubt about it: she was dead.

At first glance she appeared to be in her mid-twenties. She was wearing dark blue shorts and a white, long-sleeve shirt over a black bra, and a wrist watch—no shoes. From where I was standing, there didn't look to be a mark on her. No cuts or bruises. Her skin, a dirty gray color, told a story all its own. *Oh my, what a way to go. Hang on. I think I know her.*

I didn't go down and check. I wanted to, but if it was a crime scene, I couldn't disturb it. If not, there was nothing I could do for her anyway, and her identity could wait.

I sighed, shook my head, turned, waved the others away, then walked back to the cart, grabbed my phone, and called Kate. She answered immediately, and she wasn't happy. In fact, she sounded... angry.

Kate Gazzara, my one-time partner at the Chattanooga PD, is now a lieutenant in the Major Crimes Unit.

Me? I'm an ex-cop turned private investigator. I've known Kate for more than sixteen years, since she was a rookie. I still work with her now and then, mostly as an unpaid consultant, and much to her superiors' aggravation. They'd like to put a stop to it, but it's a match that works. And we've closed some heavy cases together, so they grudgingly sanction our collaboration.

She arrived in an unmarked police cruiser some twenty minutes later with her partner Sergeant Lonnie Guest in tow. He and I have also had our moments. We were at the police academy together. When we graduated, I moved onward and upward, but Lonnie didn't, and he holds a grudge about it to this day, though that grudge has eased somewhat over the last year. I've underestimated him in the past because he comes off as a fat, lazy slob, but I think that's a persona he purposely cultivates. It's the perpetual shit-eating grin he wears that bothers me most.

Kate, as usual, looked stunning: almost six feet tall, with a slender figure, dirty blonde hair tied in a ponytail, huge hazel eyes and a high forehead. Dressed for the weather, she had on a pair of baggy, lightweight tan pants, a white, short-sleeve blouse, a Glock 26 in a holster on her right hip, and her gold badge on her left. Lonnie, for some strange reason, was in uniform, and he had a sheepish look about him.

"Hey, Kate, Lonnie," I said as they walked toward me through the long grass.

Kate strode right past me to the edge of the embankment "What do you have?"

Whew! No hi, hello, kiss my ass, nothing. "Woman," I said. "Girl, maybe. I haven't been down there, but she's dead, I'm sure. No sign of injuries, at least from up here. I think I might know her. Not much else to tell. What the hell's up with you?"

"Not a goddamn thing a week on the beach away from this mess wouldn't cure," she said, scrambling down the bank and into the water. "I'm tired, Harry. I'm bone tired, and I hope to hell this is nothing more than an accident. I don't need another homicide. I have four to deal with already. And this." She waved her hand at Lonnie. "He goes and gets himself put back in uniform for a month. Just when I needed him most. Stupid son of a bitch." She bent down and gently touched the girl's neck, then stepped away and clambered back up the bank.

"Yeah, she's dead. I called Doc Sheddon right after you called me. He's on his way. Shouldn't be more than a minute or two. I also called CSI, so they should be here soon too."

She glared at Lonnie, then at me. "Ask him," she said. "Go on. Ask him."

I looked at Lonnie, my eyebrows raised. He grinned sheepishly, and shrugged.

"I... er, was a little rough with one of the rookies."

"A little rough. You smacked him upside the ear is

what you did. You're lucky they didn't fire you, much less put you back in uniform."

"Damn it, Kate. I didn't hit him hard. It was just a swipe. If the captain hadn't seen me do it.... Besides, it's only for a month."

I smiled. I couldn't help it. It was typical Lonnie. The proverbial bull in a china shop. Heavy handed, thoughtless, and often reckless.

"Kate, my ass," she said. "From now on you'll call me Lieutenant. Understand?"

He grinned at her, but he understood. Kate Gazzara has two distinct and separate personas. Most of the time she's the nice girl that everyone would like to date, but then there's the tough, no-nonsense, hard-ass cop that nobody dares fool around with. Guess which one it was that day.

"Hey," I said. "That looks like the doc." A golf cart was flying down the fairway at full speed, bumping and pitching at each hill and valley in the rolling terrain. The black CSI unit followed at a much more sedate speed.

Doc was driving, and having a ball, but he wasn't alone. His forensic anthropologist, Carol Owens, was hanging on for dear life.

"Whew. That was fun," he said after he'd come to a stop, and eased himself out of the cart. Carol stayed put, looking decidedly sick. "Must do that again sometime. Hey everybody. Nice day for it. Well, for us anyway. What have we got?"

Kate told him as he dragged his black case from the seat of the cart, set it down, and opened it. He looked inside, had second thoughts, walked to the riverbank, put his hands on his hips, and stared down at the body. Carol joined him, saying something I couldn't hear. He nodded and walked back to the cart, his head down, muttering under his breath.

"As I said, nice day for it." He looked up at me as he sat sideways on the cart seat. "You find this one, Harry?"

"No. I was back on the tee. Greg over there was looking for his ball; he found her."

Sheddon nodded, took off his shoes and socks, rolled up his pants. "Carol, you stay here. No point in getting your feet wet." Then he picked his way down the bank and into the water.

"Whoohoo. It's cold."

He wasn't down there but a moment or two before he came scrambling back up the bank.

"Dead!" he declared. "Don't know how or when, so don't ask. Water's cold. That will make it difficult to get an accurate time of death. Won't be able to do anything till I get her on the table. Sad. She's a pretty young thing. Can't be more than twenty-six or seven. Ambulance is on its way. I've gotta go; things to do; people to see. Tomorrow morning, Kate. Nine o'clock. Don't be late. See ya, Harry. You, too August, Larry. Hey Henry. Sorry. I didn't see you. You okay? Good, good. I'm outta here. C'mon, Carol. Bye."

He was always the same. He kind of reminded me of the White Rabbit.... No, he was more Bilbo Baggins. He was always in a hurry; never stopped talking even to take a breath. He flung his big bag onto the seat, climbed in, and then they were gone, the golf cart bumping and jumping away toward the clubhouse.

"Damn it!" Kate whispered, so low I could barely hear her. "That's all I need, a wasted morning at the Forensic Center. No. Hell no. It's not going to happen." She looked at Lonnie, shook her head. If looks could kill, Lonnie would have been no more than dust on the wind.

She looked at me. "Harry...."

"Oh no. No, no, no. I'm busy, too. I can't spare the time."

"Bullshit. You're out here fooling around with.... Oh, sorry Judge, Larry, Mr. Starke." It was like she'd just noticed them. "Well, fooling around out here abusing little white balls. It wouldn't hurt you to do me a favor. I'll fix it."

And she did. Right then and there. She called her boss, Chief Johnston. I watched as she argued; I watched as her face grew redder and redder. The chief was not in favor of the idea. But finally she turned to me and said, "Nine o'clock tomorrow morning. Don't be late, or Johnston will have my guts. Now, I need lunch, and you're buying. Here at the club, or somewhere else? You name it."

Before I could answer, the ambulance came over the rise, heading toward us. It took less than ten minutes for them to get her out of the water and into the vehicle.

Kate had a few words with the CSI team while I took a look at the body, and found out that I was right. I did know her. Doc was wrong about her age. Angela Hartwell was twenty-nine, and she would no longer grace the bar at the club, nor anywhere else. *What the hell happened to her?* Yes, I sure as hell would attend the autopsy tomorrow. I needed to know.

We all stood and watched as the ambulance slowly carried her away. There was a crowd of folks watching: our little group and Greg's, club members at the top of the rise, even a couple of greenkeepers seated on their mowers.

"I guess you guys will have to play on without me," I said, but they didn't. Their mood was as somber as mine. We turned the carts around and headed back to the clubhouse, Kate and Lonnie following in the unmarked police car.

"Let's go somewhere quiet for lunch," I said to Kate as I handed the cart and my clubs over to the attendant. "It's a zoo in there. How about Henry's on Fifty-Eighth?"

"Yeah. That'll do. Lonnie, you take the car back to the station. I'll see you later."

He wasn't happy, but he did as he was told.

2

If there's anything I hate worse than attending an autopsy, I can't think what it is. Over the years, I've seen some god-awful things in Doc Sheddon's house of horrors. The bodies of young kids, abused sexually and physically or beaten to death, victims of arson, drive-by shootings, stabbings, you name it. Teenagers dead before their time....

There was one who'd been shot in the gut at close range with a 20-guage shotgun. The hospital had tried to patch him up, but his innards had been turned into mush. He'd just turned eighteen.

There was another who'd been shot with a .45 while lying on his back on the floor. He'd tried to ward off the shot with his feet; the big slug had gone through one of them and hit him in the face just the same. You can imagine what that must have looked like. The slug, deformed by its passage through shoe leather, flesh, and bone, had exploded his head like it was a watermelon. I try to stay away from Doc Sheddon's lair, if I possibly can.

I run a successful private investigation agency—yes, I'm a PI—with offices on Georgia not far from the courts and law offices in downtown Chattanooga. From there, it's a drive of maybe ten minutes to the Forensic Center on Amnicola, less if the traffic is light. I was still late that Friday morning—only by a couple of minutes, but it was enough. Doc Sheddon wasn't in the best of moods. Overnight, the street gangs had sent him another kid. This one had been sitting in front of the TV when a bullet came through the wall and hit her in the throat. She'd bled to death in minutes. She was nine years old.

"Dammit, Harry. I said nine o'clock. It's now...." He consulted the clock on the wall. "Well, it's five after." He shook his head, heaved himself to his feet, swallowed the last of his coffee, and shambled out from behind his desk.

"I'm gonna quit this damn job one of these days. I sure as hell am." He adjusted the Glock on his hip. I always wondered why a medical examiner needed to go armed, but I guess that was just Doc. I'd always thought him a little paranoid. Hell, the first thing he did whenever he rode with me in my car, even before he put on his seat belt, was lock the door.

"Let's go take a look at her," he said, heading for the door. "You want coffee before we go in?"

I declined. He nodded, pointed to an empty locker, and then began to dress for the job. Scrub suit, vinyl apron, surgical hat, gloves, mask, eye protection, rubber boots. I did the same. By the time I was ready, he was already at the table, talking into the overhead microphone.

And there she was, all that remained of the once-vivacious Angela Hartwell.

Carol had already removed the body bag, the plastic wrap, and Angela's clothes, which were bagged and ready to be sent to the lab. She'd also washed the body, taken samples of hair from her scalp, face, eyebrows, etc.—her legs and the rest of her were clean shaven—and she'd swabbed all the orifices. The samples were labeled and stored. Finally, Carol had X-rayed her from head to toe. Angela Hartwell was now ready for the ultimate degradation.

In the absence of a morgue assistant (there was no money for one in the budget), Carol stood ready to assist the good doctor.

Once again, I was stuck by the incongruity of it all, how a living, breathing, human being could suddenly be reduced to little more than a slab of meat. Oh, the body still looks human, but somehow... well, it loses its identity, its... reality, I suppose.

Angela lay on her back, the block already under her back to extend her chest for.... Look, actually I can do without all the detail, and so can you, so I'll move right along.

Sheddon made the classic Y incision.... You know what the worst part of an autopsy is? It's when they take those damned pruning shears to the ribcage. The crunch they make is god-awful. So, Sheddon opened her chest and removed and weighed her organs, opened the skull, removed the brain and did the same and, to cut it short, came to the conclusion that she'd been strangled.

"How do you figure that?" I asked. "There are no ligature marks, no bruising or petechiae that I can see."

"Oh, there are petechiae. But it's suborbital, under the eyelids."

"Then she must have put up a fight. Is there anything under her fingernails? I don't see it, Doc. There's not a mark on her anywhere."

"Well, there actually is. See here?" He indicated a slight discoloration on her upper left bicep. "And here." This time it was the right bicep. "Pressure has been applied to both spots. Not much, I grant you, but it leads me to believe she was unconscious at the time of death."

"I see it, but—unconscious?"

"I think so. It's possible she was under the influence of Rohypnol, ketamine, or some such drug. GHB maybe, one of the so-called "date rape" drugs. If so, it wouldn't have taken much effort to do her in."

He looked at me, shook his head, and said, "Harry, you know as well as I do what goes on these days. Here's what I think may have happened. Someone slipped her the proverbial Mickey, then straddled her, placing his or her knees on her arms, here, to make sure she didn't move. Then whoever it was simply applied gentle pressure to the carotid arteries, thus starving the brain of oxygen. Total loss of consciousness would have occurred within ten to fifteen seconds, death within three to four minutes."

"Gentle pressure? Are you kidding me?"

"No. Ten to twelve pounds of force is all it would

take, especially if the victim was in a state of torpor due to the ingestion of, say, ketamine."

"You're sure, then, that it was manual strangulation?"

"Of that, yes. I won't be able to confirm the drug, or even if there was one, until the toxicology comes back, and that could take several weeks. In the meantime, I suggest you assume that I'm right—I usually am—and conduct your investigation accordingly."

It was said without a hint of self-consciousness. The doctor was well aware of his abilities and, as always, was willing to stand on his beliefs and opinions until he was proven wrong. He rarely was.

"Time of death?" I asked.

"Ah, now that's a tricky one. She wasn't wearing much in the way of clothing, so that wouldn't have slowed the rate of drop in body temperature. The water was 58.4 degrees, and the body temperature taken when she came in yesterday morning was 79.2. There's some rigor mortis, but not much. Lividity? She must have been mostly on her back after she died, because lividity is well-established, as you can see," he gave the girl's buttock a poke. "So at least eight to ten hours. Taking all that into consideration.... I can't be absolutely precise, but I'd say that when you found her, she'd been dead for ten to twelve hours."

"So, late on Wednesday evening then? Between nine o'clock and midnight?"

"I'd say that's about right. Probably closer to ten o'clock than midnight, with eleven being the prime number," he said with a grin, but then he shook his head clicked his tongue against the roof of his mouth. "It was pre-meditated, personal, and brutal. Whoever did this to her must have hated her very much."

"Was she killed where we found her, or dumped there after her death?"

"Lividity suggests she was killed on the spot, but I don't think so. Look here." He pointed to her left wrist. This is where she wore her watch. There's some discoloration there, too, and here on her right ankle." He stared at the body, seemingly lost in thought. I looked at the wrist and ankle. The bruising on the wrist was barely discernable; I couldn't see it on the ankle at all, but if Doc said it was there, it was.

"And...?" I prompted.

"I'm thinking that the discoloration might have been caused by pressure. Look, suppose someone – two some-ones – picked her up by her wrists and ankles, to carry her, perhaps. That would have put pressure on the watch causing it to dig in and cause bruising. The discoloration on the ankle is slight, so... it's difficult to say. Maybe she was grabbed by the wrists and dragged, by just one person. If so, that might account for the lack of shoes. They could have slipped off as she was being dragged.... If she *was* dumped, it would have had to have been within an hour of death, two at the most."

He was silent for a moment, then turned, stripped off his gloves, and said, "Anything else? No? Good luck to you, Harry boy. You'll need it."

"Well at least we have something to work with, and we know who she is. So that's a good start. I'll pass it all on to Kate Gazzara. It's her baby. I'm just here to get the skinny. Anything else I should know, Doc?"

He thought for a moment, shrugged, then shook his head. "Not that I can think of. If I do think of anything, I'll give you a buzz. In the meantime, I'll send Kate a preliminary report. The results of the toxicology... two, maybe three weeks."

I nodded, thanked him, stripped off the scrubs and the rest of the gear, and left him muttering to himself. Carol waved goodbye.

To say I was depressed was putting it mildly. I knew Angela Hartwell. In fact, I'd known her for several years. Her husband, Regis, now deceased, had been a member of the club. She retained the membership after he died.

I wonder.... We never did figure that out, did we? There was always some question about that, his death. He was a banker. Died of a heart attack. Hell, he was only thirty-eight years old. Fit as a damn fiddle. Induced, maybe? SUX or potassium chloride? Who knows. He was too young and too fit. Well, I would have thought he was, but what do I know?

I sat in my car outside the forensic center for several minutes, daydreaming. I was in another world, but not for long. My Bluetooth cut into the music playing on the radio. It was Kate.

"Hey you," I said. "What's the haps?"

"You out of there yet?"

"Just a few minutes ago. I was going to drop by and give you the good word. Where are you?"

"The Boathouse. You want to join me for lunch?"

"I can do that." I looked at my watch. It was eleven thirty. "Give me about five minutes. Order for me, will you? Get me a bowl of gumbo."

Traffic was light, so the ride to Riverfront Parkway was quick and uneventful. By a quarter to eleven I was seated across from Kate, sipping on a Blue Moon and gazing out the window. As usual, she was easy on the eye. Jeans and a white blouse. Her hair was tied back in a ponytail.

"So," she said, "how did it go?"

I filled her in on what little detail I had and wished her good luck with it, but she wasn't having it.

"I told you I was swamped. We're short-handed, Lonnie is back on the street for a month, and I just don't have the time. I do have you, however, and I managed to talk the chief into letting you consult, but I can tell you, he didn't like it worth a damn, so don't let me down."

"Consult? That means I get to do all the work. Kate. I can't do it. I'm swamped, too. I have...."

"Oh hell, Harry. Suck it up. It's not like I ask much of you. I'm always there when you need me. Now I need a favor. And it should be simple enough, right?" She didn't wait for me to answer, but continued, "And then there's the fact that you know these people. They're your kind; the country club crowd. They'll respond to you when they won't to me."

I leaned back in my seat and looked at her. She was lovely—serious as hell, but lovely. I shook my head, exasperated. I really didn't like it, but....

"Okay. Okay. I'll see what I can do—but if it gets complicated, Kate, I'm dumping it right back in your lap. I'm not a cop anymore. I left the force eight years ago to get away from this type of work, and all the stupid rules and politics, the bullshit. You know that. Now you want.... Oh hell."

She grinned at me over the rim of her glass and then sucked on her straw.

"You love it," she said. "You know you do. If it wasn't for me, you'd go nuts with all that white-collar crap you handle. Thank you, Harry. I'll make it up to you. I promise." She looked at me through her eyelashes as she said it.

Damn, she knows how to push my buttons.

There was a time when those words would have sent my heart flying, but those times were, unfortunately, long gone, and it was my fault. For more than ten years, Kate and I had been much more than friends and colleagues, until... well, that's another story. Whatever. I gave her a wan smile.

"So where will you begin?" she asked as the waiter set my gumbo down in front of me.

"With the basics. What else? Who? Where? What? When? How? I know who she is and when she died, but that's about it. I'll get Tim started on the research when I get back to the office."

Tim is one of my staff, an IT expert, a computer geek, whatever. He's been with me since before he dropped out of college when he was seventeen—yeah, he's that good— and he was a hacker way before that.

"Tell me something, Kate. I seem to recall that her husband was a banker, and that he died kinda suddenly a year ago, maybe a little more. Did you hear anything about that?"

"No. I don't recall anything. Why? What's so strange

about a sudden death? It happens all the time. Heart attack, stroke, aneurysm."

"True, but this guy was thirty-eight and a fitness freak. Worked out every day, as I recall. But you heard nothing about it?"

She shook her head, sipped another spoonful of gumbo, and looked up at me over the spoon. Then she froze. "Oh no. Don't you even go there. This is about her, not him. Harry. It's supposed to be quick and easy. Remember?"

I sucked air in through my teeth. "Yeah... but...."

"No buts, Harry. Angela Hartwell. That's it. We put it to bed, and quickly.... Oh shit. Here we go. I know that look on your face. That's what I get when I involve you. Damn it."

I grinned at her. She was right, of course. My brain was already starting to churn. Two sudden deaths. Husband and wife. A year apart? Well... wouldn't you be intrigued?

"No worries. I'll just do a little checking. Just to make sure. Probably nothing to it."

"Hah." She dropped her spoon into the empty bowl, sat back in her chair, and stared at me.

Now that's unfair. She knows I never could resist those eyes.

"You hang me out to dry, Harry," she said quietly, "and it will be the last time you do. I'm just about fed up with you making something out of nothing. Angela Hartwell. We sort it out and we put it away. Understand?'

I nodded. "Time to go," I said, avoiding her eye and rising to my feet. "Your treat, right?"

"The hell it is. Dig out that fat wallet of yours and consider yourself lucky I let you buy me lunch."

She pushed her chair back and stood up. "Angela Hartwell. No more, no less." And with that, she stalked off out of the dining room, her heels clicking sharply on the wood floor. She really did have a nice....

I dropped two twenties on the table and headed back to my office.

3

Friday May 27 – PM – My Office

It was just after one o'clock when I got back to my office that afternoon. Bob wasn't back from lunch, but the rest of my staff were all busily going about their duties.

Jacque, my long-time PA, glared at me, but said nothing. She did, however, thrust a wad of papers at me as I walked past her desk to my office.

Now, I don't want you to get the wrong idea about her. I expect a lot from her. She, in turn, expects a lot from me. She also has to deal with my moods and disrespect for detail on a daily basis. She's twenty-seven years old but looks nineteen, and has a master's degree in business administration and a bachelor's in criminology: quite a combination, which is one of the reasons I hired her even before she got out of college. But more than that, I liked her. She's Jamaican, and has an infectious personality. When she cracks a smile, she lights up the room, and she has a great sense of humor when she's not cranky with me. But she can be serious when she needs to be, especially when she's at the office.

I grabbed the pile and tilted my head to indicate she was to follow me. She closed the door behind her and seated herself on the other side of my desk.

I dumped the papers off to one side. She frowned, got up, grabbed them, and set them squarely down in front of me, not saying a single word.

"Okay, Jacque. I get it. Look, I need some space in my schedule. I need to work a murder. How busy am I?"

Now that might seem like a stupid question, with an answer I should know, right? Wrong. I stay busy, and I'm not the most organized manager in the world, as she will readily tell you. My day starts around eight o'clock, and never seems to really end. It all takes a lot of keeping up with, hence the need and question for Jacque.

"Very. You are personally handling three cases, overseeing a dozen more, and you have six potential new clients, all important, all awaiting your call."

"I knew that!" *The hell I did.*

You'll understand now why I was so reluctant to let Kate railroad me into taking on the Hartwell murder. I employ nine people, including five investigators, two secretaries, an intern, and Jacque. I run a very successful, busy agency.

There are several reasons why I'm so successful. The first is that I'm discreet—what I learn stays between me and my clients.

Second: I know just about everyone that matters, not only in Chattanooga, but also in Atlanta, Birmingham, and Nashville, not the least of whom is my father, August. It's not what you know, but who you know, right?

Third: I'm a winner. Since I first opened my doors, I have worked for just about every important lawyer and judge south of the Kentucky border, and more than a few of our city's most prominent residents. In all but a few cases, I've produced results.

Finally, over the past two years, I'd achieved a certain national notoriety, having put away a powerful United States congressman for life, for solving a decade old cold murder case, and for shedding light on the dirty secrets of human trafficking. All of which brings me a lot of business.

"Look, Jacque," I said, as I picked up the pile of paperwork. "You can handle most of this. I know you can. I trust your judgment. Make the calls, get the information, make the decisions, and tie it all up. Whatever you decide, I'll back you. If you need signatures, fine. As to my cases, I'll hand Webber off to Heather. I'll need to bring her up to speed, but that shouldn't take long. Bob can take over Jamison. He's already familiar with it, and it should be wrapping up pretty soon.

"That leaves me with Elizabeth Roe's missing son, correct?"

She nodded, expressionless.

"I'll handle that one myself. How does that sound?"

"We'll see. I'm not sure Heather is up to handling Webber... but we'll see."

I could tell she didn't like it. When she gets stressed, angry, or pressured, her Jamaican accent becomes just a little more discernable, the way it was right now.

"We'll both keep an eye on it, but she's experienced and damned good at what she does and.... I mean hell, Jacque. I can't do it all myself. That's why I hired these people. Gotta let 'em run, do their thing."

She nodded.

"Okay then. If you'll start the ball rolling," I said, handing her the pile of papers, "I need a few minutes with Tim. Would you send him in, please?"

When I said Tim was geeky, I meant it. He's tall, skinny, wears glasses, and speaks a language only he and his peers can understand—but oh boy does he know his way around a computer. He maintains the company website, handles background checks and skip searches, finds people, addresses, phone numbers, you name it. You cannot hide from Tim. He's also the busiest member of my staff.

He came in, loaded up as usual with a laptop, iPad, and iPhone. I looked at him and shook my head. He grinned at me, sat down, dumped the iPad and phone on the edge of my desk, and sat there looking at me expectantly, his hair hanging over his eyes.

"Tim. I need to know everything there is to know about a guy named Regis Hartwell. He was a local community banker. He died just over a year ago. I also need to know about his wife, Angela. We found her body in the river yesterday morning. I need to know about their social lives—real and virtual. I need to know about their business lives, who their friends were, hobbies, financials, reputations, everything—and I need it fast, so drop everything and spend the rest of the day on it. But before you do anything else, I need to know where she lived."

"You got it, Boss. If it's all local, it shouldn't be a problem."

"Good." I looked at my watch. It was just after one thirty. "Okay, go get to it. I'll expect something before close of day." And he went.

I spent the next hour with Bob Ryan, my lead investigator, and Heather Stillwell, one of two senior investigators. I brought them up to speed on the two cases I was handing off to them, and then I grabbed a cup of coffee—Dark Italian Roast, my favorite—closed my office door, and sat back down behind my desk.

I sipped on the coffee for a few moments, lost in thought. I kept seeing Angela's body, lying on its back in the shallow waters of the Tennessee.

Why there? I wondered. It's remote, yes; more than a half-mile from the clubhouse or nearest road. Easier access to the river than anywhere else on the golf course. But whoever dumped her sure as hell wasn't trying to hide her, and it couldn't have been easy getting there. Might have been seen, even late at night, after dark; there are people in the clubhouse until after midnight most nights... although, most of them are usually a little under the weather.

And then there's that 'gentle strangulation' thing. That's really weird: nasty, malicious, deliberate.

And then there's Regis Hartwell. I have a feeling.... Hell, who knows? But if he was murdered, that throws a whole different light on Angela's murder. If he was, they have to be connected. Too much of a coincidence not to be. Oh shit. What the hell have I let myself in for?

I took a sip of coffee. The cup was empty.

I went to get another one, and nearly ran into Tim, who was about to knock on my door. He had an address. She'd lived in the Mountain Shadows subdivision off Banks Road. I knew that area. It was where Tom Sattler had lived. I'd solved that case last August. I went back into my office and called Amanda.

"Hello, Harry. You taking me out tonight?" *I swear that woman is a mind reader*.

"Hah, how did you know? I thought we'd go to the club, have a nice dinner, a drink or two, and then we can go back to my place and you can stay over, if you want to."

"Dinner sounds good.... Stay over? Let me think about it." I could hear the smile in her voice. "Okay. We can do that."

"Terrific. Look, I have a couple of things to do before I can get free. How about I pick you up at your place around seven, seven thirty?"

"Seven thirty is good. That will give me time to get home and cleaned up after the six o'clock broadcast."

Oh, and does she ever clean up.

4

I found Angela Hartwell's house. It was on Misty Mountain Trail, just off Royal Mountain Drive. It was a nice property: two stories with an attached two-car garage on maybe a half an acre, just what you might expect of a successful banker. The place was deserted, which was also what I'd expected. I'd already called Kate and told her I was going to take a look at it— concerned neighbors tend to be overzealous in these upscale subdivisions.

I parked the Maxima and took a walk around the home. Everything was as it should be. The lawns were mowed, the flowerbeds full and colorful, the bushes neatly trimmed. Angela had cared about her home.

At the back of the house, I went up the steps onto the deck, took out my set of picks, and opened the back door.

The door opened into a mud room that gave way to the kitchen, and from there to a spacious living room dominated by a stone fireplace. Past that was a large office, and then the master bedroom and bathroom.

There were three more bedrooms and two bathrooms—one with access on either side—on the upper floor, and several family rooms in the basement. Everything was spick and span—but too spick and span. It looked as if the place hadn't been lived in for months. Oh, there were clothes hanging in the closet of the master bedroom, all women's, but that was all. The house was fully furnished, but the rest of the closets were empty.

The desk in the office was clean, the drawers and credenza... yep, you guessed it: empty. No computer, just a phone. The whole place was pristine. There was one way to find out if she'd lived there recently, though.

I locked and closed the door behind me and then walked across the lawns to the house next door, rang the bell, and waited.

The woman who answered the door was tall, almost as tall as me. True, she was wearing heels, but still. She was about thirty, wearing yoga pants and a sports bra under one of those tank tops that covers everything yet somehow manages to show it all, with a low neckline and wide-open arm holes. *With heels?*

"Yes, what do you want?" *Cryptic, too!*

"My name is Harry Starke." I flashed my badge. "I'm an investigator. I've just been to the Hartwell home next door. There doesn't seem to be anyone living there. Would you happen to know where I could find Mrs. Hartwell?"

"Well, you're right. She doesn't live there. She hasn't since her husband died. Why do you want her?"

"It's just an enquiry. I need to ask her some questions. Do you know where I could find her?"

"Let me see that badge again." She held out her hand. I sighed and handed it to her.

"You're not a cop. What the hell are you after? I'm going to call the police." She started to close the door. She didn't offer to return the badge. I put a hand on the door. She pushed harder.

"Hold on a minute, Mrs.—whatever your name is. I'm working with the Major Crimes Division at the Chattanooga P.D. Here. Call this number, and give me my badge." I handed her Kate's card. She took it from me, scrutinized it, took out a cell phone and dialed the number. The call took less than thirty seconds, during which time she stared at me, her face growing more relaxed as the call progressed. Finally, she ended the call and smiled at me.

"I'm sorry, Mr. Starke. A girl can't be too careful these days, can she? I'm Clara, Clara Mackie. Please. Do come in."

She turned and walked away into the house, her hips swinging—those really were tight pants. I wonder if she has any idea what that does to a guy. *And she's worried about being too careful?*

"Please, sit down." She waved a hand at the breakfast table. "Can I get you some iced tea, lemonade, water?"

"Er... no. No thank you. I won't take up too much of your time, I promise."

"Oh, it's no trouble at all. How can I help you?"

Is this the same woman who answered the door?

She sat opposite me, put her elbows on the table, lapped one hand over the other, and rested her chin on them.

"Now I know who you are. You're on TV all the time. You're famous, Mr. Starke."

"Not so much, Mrs. Mackie. Look, I'd better tell you: Mrs. Hartwell is dead. Murdered. We found her body in the river by the golf course yesterday morning...."

"Oh my God. No!" She sat bolt upright. Horrified. "What happened? Who did it? Who killed her?"

"That's what I'm trying to find out. And to do that I need to know where she was living, because it certainly wasn't in the house next door."

"Oh my God. I can't believe it. First Regis then Angela." She wiped away tears.

"She has... she had an apartment. She couldn't stand the house without him, without Regis. It's one of those nice places in Cobblestone Heights, number 33. Let me give you her iPhone number." She grabbed a scrap of paper, wrote the number on it, then handed it to me.

"She still keeps some things here—next door, that is—but I know she'd decided she wanted to sell the house. She just couldn't bring herself to do it."

She sniffed, wiped her cheeks with a tissue, looked across the table at me, screwed up her eyes, and shuddered.

I made a note of the address. "What about friends?" I asked.

"Lots. He was a banker. They were always socializing. Until he died, that is. Then... well, she just withdrew."

"Any close friends in particular?"

She thought for a moment, nodded, and said, "There were the Bentleys. Me and Joe, of course; Joe's my husband. He's in real estate. The Crofts... and Ben and Joan Loftis. Those are the ones that come to mind, but there were many more. He moved among the financial elite, and they were members of the Country Club. Very social."

I looked at my watch. It was almost three o'clock, and I wanted to see the apartment. It wasn't too far away, maybe ten minutes. So I thanked her, said goodbye, and left her standing at the door looking miserable.

When I got back into my car, I hit the Bluetooth and called Jacque to let her know I wouldn't be back into the office that afternoon, and then I headed south on Banks toward East Brainerd.

Cobblestone Heights was an upscale, three-story complex, walled and gated. The guard was amiable enough, but protective of his charge, until I showed him my card and offered him a twenty, which he took with all the dexterity of a stage magician.

The gate swung open, and I drove on through. Number 33 was a ground-floor unit on the west side of the block, overlooking the pool.

My lock picks made short work of the front door, and I soon found myself in a world I certainly hadn't expected. I think it must have been junky to begin with, but the place had been turned over, and whoever had done it hadn't been bothered about making a mess, which told me that whoever it was hadn't been concerned about being disturbed or discovered. They knew Angela wasn't coming back.

There wasn't a square inch that hadn't been searched, turned in some cases literally upside down.

That told me they hadn't found what they were looking for, and that frustrated the hell out of me. I wanted to get in there and search for myself, but I couldn't. This was a crime scene. I heaved a sigh, stepped backward out of the front door, reached around and locked it, then pulled it closed.

I called Kate and told her to get a CSI unit out there, and then I went and warned the guard not to let anyone near the apartment. I sat in my car, lay my head back on the rest, and tried to think. It wasn't happening. My head was in a whirl. I needed time, space, a pen, and paper. I needed to go back to the office.

It was almost four-thirty when I arrived. It was Friday evening, so most of the crew had already left. Only Jacque and Tim remained. I told Jacque I would lock up and that she was to go home and enjoy her weekend, which I knew she would anyway. She and her partner Lucy always do. Tim I had join me in my office.

With his laptop under his arm and a sheaf of printouts in his hand, Tim sat down opposite my desk, opened a file, and waited while I went to the cabinet and poured myself a small Laphroaig scotch whisky over a single ice cube.

"Okay," I said. "What do we have?'

"I'll start with Angela, because there's not a whole lot I could find out about her. She led a quiet life after her husband died. She was well off; I haven't been able to get a financial report yet, but I got a credit score. 832. Almost perfect. As for her net worth... I haven't been able to find out, yet, but it's probably substantial. She owned the house, but rented the apartment. She sat on several charitable boards, but was not actively involved in any of them after Regis Hartwell died. That's about it as far she's concerned."

"Okay, how about her husband?"

"Regis Hartwell died of a heart attack on Sunday March 29, 2015, just over a year ago. He was a banker. He owned and operated Hartwell Community Banks. There were nine of them: three in Chattanooga, one in South Pittsburg, two in Cleveland, two in Dalton, and one in Fort Oglethorpe. They're a privately held company, so I haven't been able get an estimate of their value. I'll keep on digging. When Regis died, the company passed to his younger brother, Ralph. He was the senior vice president of the company, but since it was privately held, he owned no part of it. Regis was the sole owner. Ralph Hartwell is thirty-eight years old, married, has two young kids, lives on Signal Mountain. Angela inherited the family home and all of her husband's personal assets. Right now, that's all I have. It's not much. Sorry."

"So Regis had a brother, and *he* inherited the banks, not Angela?"

"Yes."

"Hm. Could be a motive right there. Okay, Tim. Go on home. We'll talk again Monday morning. Have a good weekend."

He closed the door behind him, and I settled down to think.

I took a pad from the desk drawer and began to write. I have an iPad, but I can't cope with that stupid digital keyboard, nor do I like to use a laptop. I like to do it the old fashioned way: paper and pencil. I thought for a moment, then started to write.

Subject

Angela "Angela" Hartwell - Deceased

29 years old

Husband—Regis—Dead at thirty-eight—2015 C.O.D —Suspicious

T.O.D.—11PM Thursday May 26

Questions

1. Where was she during the hours before her death?
2. Who did she spend them with?
3. Who benefits from her death? Ralph Hartwell????
4. Who would have reason to kill her?
5. Did she have enemies?
6. What about her husband?
7. Is her death connected to his?
8. Who were her close friends? Clara & Joe Mackie; Luis & Ester Bentley; Michael & Laura Croft; Ben & Joan Loftis. Any more?
9. Do they have alibis?
10. Did she have a boyfriend/girlfriend?
11. She did, said, or saw something that caused her death. What was it?
12. Someone searched her apartment. What were they looking for?
13. Where are her small personal items, shoes, make up and such? There were none found

near the body... unless (call Kate. See if CSI found anything at the apartment)

14. Where is her cell phone? Women never go anywhere without one.

15. Where's her car? Need to check that.

I sat there, my brain churning the way it always does when I see in black and white what little I have.

I looked at the list. Fifteen questions just for starters, and all I really had was a name, a crime scene—what little there was of it—an approximate time of death, an empty house, a ransacked apartment, and... that was it. I realized that even though I'd know her for years, I knew absolutely nothing about the woman other than her age. *Damn it.*

I looked at my watch. It was already after five thirty. I needed to wrap things up and get out of there.

I went out into the main office, made a dozen copies of my subject sheet, folded one and put it into my wallet, dropped the rest of them into Jacque's inbox, then went back into my office and slid into my black Nike golf jacket. It was warm outside, but I like to cover the Smith & Wesson M&P9 on my hip. Finally, I set the security system and left the office.

I arrived home, a condo on Lakeshore Lane, some fifteen minutes later. It was almost six. I was due to pick Amanda up at seven thirty, so I had a little more than an hour to get myself ready. That meant I could manage just one more small Laphroaig, which I did.

5

B y seven, I was showered and dressed in what I call my IBM rig: dark gray slacks, Gucci loafers, a pale blue shirt with a royal blue tie, and a navy blue blazer. It's not really me, but it's comfortable and the folks at the club can live with it, and the jacket nicely covers the shoulder holster and M&P9 under my left arm. I never go anywhere without it. I even carry it in my golf bag out on the course. Paranoid? Maybe, but I'm only alive today because I carry it with me at all times.

I made it to Amanda's a couple of minutes early and let myself in—she'd given me the key for my birthday a couple of months ago. Some gift, huh?

She was in the bathroom, dressed but not quite ready. She was putting on mascara. I leaned against the bathroom doorjamb and watched. You know, I've never met a guy who didn't think his girlfriend was the most beautiful thing on two legs, but Amanda... she really is.

She wore her strawberry-blond hair bobbed, elfin-like. Her heart-shaped face was defined by high cheekbones, a small, slightly upturned nose and huge, wide-set, pale green eyes. She was wearing a simple, sleeveless pale blue dress cut an inch above her knees, and matching heels. I watched as she leaned over the vanity and applied a touch of pale pink lipstick. There were times when I wondered if life was worth the living, especially when I was faced with such tragic events as those of the past two days. But then there were times when I felt blessed. This was one of them.

"Whaaat?" she asked, past the lipstick. "Stop staring at me, Harry. You're making me nervous."

I was making *her* nervous? What the hell did she think she was doing to me?

"C'mere." I grabbed her arm and pulled her to me. She dropped the lipstick on the vanity, put her arms around me, and leaned away from me, laughing, her upper thighs pressing against mine.

"Stop it. You'll smoosh me." She leaned in, kissed me lightly on the lips, and pushed me away. "Wow. You're in a good mood."

She was right. I was. But hell, who wouldn't be? I was going to spend the next forty-eight hours with a stunningly beautiful woman, who adored me and was willing to make it plain to anyone who cared to listen. And once again, I was struck by the incongruity of it. Less than a year ago, I'd hated this woman with a passion. I couldn't stand the sight of her, but now I hated every moment I wasn't with her. Well, that might be a bit of an exaggeration, but you get the idea.

In case you're wondering... well, I've already mentioned that Amanda is an anchor at Channel 7 TV. It was almost three years ago that she did an on-air profile of me—I'd just solved a major cold case. Anyway, the profile was less than flattering, although she'll tell you different. Truthfully it was a hatchet job, and I swore she'd never get the chance to do it again. Then, back in August of last year, she managed to talk me into a "collaboration," as she called it. One thing led to another, and here we are. Funny how things change.

It was Friday night, so the club was packed with members when we arrived. No matter. I'd taken the precaution of calling ahead to book my favorite table, the one in the bay window overlooking the ninth green.

It must have taken us at least twenty minutes to get from the foyer to the table. One after another the club members grabbed either Amanda or me to say hello and have a word or two of conversation.

As a newscaster, she was used to it. I'm not. In fact I hate it. But I'm now almost as well-known as she is. I've gained a certain notoriety over the past several years, which isn't good in my line of business. Oh, it brings me lots of business, but it also makes me something of a target.

"Whew," she whispered as we sat down. "That was an ordeal. Whose idea was it to come here on a Friday night?"

The question was rhetorical, and required no answer, so I didn't. I just took her hand under the table and squeezed it. She smiled up at me. Life was good.

I ordered drinks. A gin and tonic for me—Bombay Sapphire—and a Yellow Bird for Amanda—something she'd discovered and enjoyed on our trip to Jamaica at

Christmas. The drinks came, and we were still talking about nothing in particular. I wanted to talk to her about the Hartwells, but now was not the time.

"Hello, you two. I have someone here who'd like to meet you."

I looked up, startled. We both did. "Hello, Dad." I stood and offered him my hand. It was always like that. My father is an ex-marine colonel and he still retained his somewhat formal posture, even with me, but that wasn't what got my attention. He was accompanied by a woman. Or a goddess.

She stood at least six foot four in her heels, an inch taller than my father. I was immediately struck by her likeness to Heather Nauert, a news anchor for the Fox News Channel, but this girl was taller, more broad-shouldered. She had the same blonde hair, cut pageboy style, and she was dressed in a clinging white sheath that accentuated every curve in her body.

Ouch! I almost said it out loud. Amanda had kicked me.

"Harry, Amanda," August said, "this is Ruth Archer. Ruth, meet Amanda Cole and my son, Harry Starke."

I offered my hand. She took it. Her grip was... strong.

"Nice to meet you, Mr. Starke. I've heard so much about you." She turned her head slightly so that she was looking down at Amanda, who had remained seated. "You, too. Ms. Cole. I so enjoy watching you on television."

Amanda nodded, and gifted her with an icy smile.

"Would you like to join us for a drink?" I asked, knowing damned well I would suffer for it later.

"Well, just a quick one, then." It was my father who accepted the invitation.

And they both sat. August next to Amanda, Ruth rather a little too close to me.

"I wanted to meet you, Harry…. May I call you, Harry?"

"Of course." I could feel Amanda's fingernails digging into my thigh.

"Well, Harry, I wanted to meet you because I've heard so much about you, on television and all, and I'm simply fascinated by what you do."

The nails dug deeper.

"Ruth is a local businesswoman, Harry," my father said. "I'm sure you've heard of the Archer Group. Yes?"

I nodded. I had indeed heard of it. Who hadn't?

"She plays golf, too. Don't you Ruth? She's something of a hustler. Took fifty off me today."

She smiled. I smiled. It was a rare thing for my father to lose, to anyone, let alone a lovely creature like this.

"August tells me you play, too, Harry. Maybe you'd like to play with me one day." It was not what she said but how she said it. Amanda's claws drew blood.

"Oh, you'd better watch it, Harry boy," my father said. "Ruth was State High School Champion in '95, and a member of the varsity team at Stamford. She has a two handicap, and she'll take you to the cleaners."

Ruth lowered her head and smiled modestly at me. I had to move Amanda's hand. Ruth noticed.

"Look. I'm so sorry. We're spoiling your evening together. August, I'll let you buy me another drink at the bar, and then I have to go home. Saturday's a big day at the dealership."

They said their goodbyes and left, and I was glad to see them go. My thigh was killing me. I hadn't known Amanda had such a strong grip.

"Geeze, that was uncalled for," I said, rubbing my thigh."

"Maybe you'd like to play with me one day," she mimicked. It wasn't a bad imitation, either, and I couldn't help but laugh.

"Why, Amanda, darling. I do believe you're jealous."

"Oh come on, Harry. One, she's as phony as a three-dollar bill, and two, she's not your type. She's also a dangerous bitch. I know her well, even if she doesn't know me. Charlie Grove knows her too, and the rest of her family. According to him, they've been screwing the public ever since old man Archer died back in 2002."

Charlie Grove is an interesting character. He's Channel 7's resident consumer watchdog, a loudmouth, and one nosey son of a bitch. He has a laugh like a hyena and personality to match. I've often wondered how come someone hadn't removed him from the land of the living long ago; he was that unpopular. He was, however, extremely good at what he did. They called him Pit Bull Charlie because, like a dog with a bone, he never gave up. A single consumer complaint and Channel 7's dog of war was ready to take on any and all, individual, businesses, large or small. Just a hint that Charlie was sniffing around was usually all it took to bring justice to the masses. He was a nasty little creep, but he got the job done and brought in the ratings.

. . .

Now I was interested. If Amanda was correct, what the hell did Ruth Archer with me, or August for that matter? And she was right, the woman wasn't my type—or my father's. I waved to Joe and ordered more drinks.

"Tell me about her," I said.

"Why are you interested? Should I be worried?"

"Hell, no. I'm just curious, is all."

So she told me.

"Jack Archer owned and operated a small used car dealership on Rossville Boulevard. His cars were cheap, and he toted the note. Revenue was small but steady, and his business was very profitable, mostly because no one ever defaulted on a loan. People who tried it got their legs broken, or worse."

She took a sip of her yellow drink, then continued.

"Jack started the company more than thirty years ago, selling singles out of his garage. He toted the note even then. You know the saying, right? 'From little acorns....' Anyway, he made the move to Rossville Boulevard and business improved, and then he died, in a car wreck. He was only fifty-two. Ruth was twenty-five and fresh out of university, and she took over the business. She met James Fletcher while she was at Stanford and married him a year after her father died. The marriage lasted about six months. Since then the dealership's grown into a group of companies that include a high-end used car dealership, a used boat brokerage, a real estate company, and a finance company—it makes loans only within the company, to its customers." She took another sip of her drink.

"Ruth has two sisters, twins, Rachel and Rebekah. They were still in college when their father died in 2002. They were twenty-one. They both graduated a year later with degrees in finance from the University of Georgia. Rachel runs the real estate and finance companies; Rebekah runs the dealership and the boat brokerage. Ruth oversees it all."

"How the hell do you know all that," I asked.

She smiled. "I told you: Charlie's had them in his sights for years. He does good work. You know that."

I did indeed. "Pit Bull Charlie Grove," I said, dryly. How is that nasty little son of a bitch?"

She chuckled, "He doesn't like you, either. He likes me, though. He's fine."

"Look," I said, taking her hand, and glancing surreptitiously down to see if there was blood under her fingernails. There wasn't. "We came here for a nice night out. Let's forget about it, and about Ruth, and about my father. We have the whole weekend ahead of us. Let's enjoy it."

"Fine with me. But the next time you look at another woman like that, Harry Starke, there *will* be blood under my fingernails."

Damn, the woman never misses a trick.

We left the club early. Well, earlier than usual. I'd had enough of the noise—and the constant attention we both were getting. Besides, I couldn't get Angela

Hartwell out of my head. The few times I remembered seeing her, talking to her, I'd been impressed with her vitality, but that had been before her husband died. I'd seen her only a couple of times since, and those just in passing. Somehow, though, all of the visions of the past, the vitality, the energy, the quiet beauty, and finally the sadness, had all been replaced by the image of that pale body lying face-up in the shallow waters of the Tennessee. It was depressing as hell, and I just wanted to go home.

6

W e arrived back at my condo on Lakeshore Lane a little after eleven.

"Hey, let me do it," Amanda said, taking the bottle of Laphroaig and the Waterford glass from my hands. She poured a generous three fingers into the glass and dropped in a single ice cube. I took it from her and touched her lips with mine, then took a sip, put my head back, closed my eyes, and savored the slow burn as it slid down my throat.

I opened my eyes. She was laughing at me.

"I've never seen anyone enjoy a drink like you do," she said.

"Ah, but you see, it's not a drink. It's an... an out-of-body, unworldly experience. One that very few can understand. A taste for exquisite scotch whiskey has to be cultivated and refined. To have such a taste is to be able to experience one of the finer things in life. Do you realize that it took the Scotts more than 400 years to perfect it?"

"No, I didn't, and I hate the nasty stuff. How you can guzzle it the way you do beats me."

"*Nasty stuff?* C'mere." I put the glass down, grabbed her by the waist, and pulled her to me. She was giggling like a little girl. Two minutes later, she wasn't. Two minutes later, she was gasping for breath, and I was doing the grinning, that and sipping on the nectar of the gods.

I poured her a glass of Niersteiner, took her hand, and guided her gently over to the sofa in front of the big windows.

"Isn't she beautiful?"

"She? Who are you talking about?" Amanda looked at me, her eyes scrunched up.

"The river. Isn't she beautiful? She's like a beautiful woman: mysterious, moody, vibrant, unpredictable, sometimes turbulent, sometimes calm, sometimes deadly, always secretive. Like you, Amanda."

"Hah, so you say." She sipped her wine and stared out into the darkness.

"I do say. You are all of those things and more." I put my arm around her; she laid her head on my shoulder. I could tell she was mulling it over.

"You make her sound like a mistress."

"In many ways, that's exactly what she is. I fell in love with her the day I bought this place. I had the old windows replaced with these floor-to-ceiling units, so I could better connect with her. She's always here, waiting for me, sometimes sleeping, sometimes angry, always... alive. Look at her now. What does she say to you?"

"She tells me you're one creepy son of a bitch," she laughed.

"Ah, you don't get it...."

"Oh, but I do. I understand completely. And I envy you. She's everything you could want in a lover, and then some. I could be jealous, Harry."

"Jealous? You? Hah! You, my darling, have nothing to be jealous about. At this very moment, you hold my heart tightly in your cold and clammy little hands." And she did.

"That's not true, Harry. You're your own man; always have been, always will be. Nobody will ever tie you down."

I thought about that. Maybe she was right. I was forty-three years old, a confirmed bachelor, and I had no desire to change my status, as they say on Facebook.

She had her feet drawn up onto the sofa, her head on my chest, her hands clasped around the glass. I said nothing.

"Harry?"

"What?"

"Oh... nothing."

"Come on. Out with it."

"No, some other time. Let's go to bed."

And we did.

7

I awoke early the following morning, Saturday. I hadn't slept a whole lot. Amanda? She'd slept like a dead dog, barely moving the entire night. I got up twice, wandered around the living room, went back to bed, and finally gave it up. Angela Hartwell had me by the shorts and wouldn't let go.

I made coffee, Dark Italian Roast which, like good scotch whiskey, is an acquired taste. I took a cup into the bedroom and placed it on the nightstand beside Amanda. and looked down at her. *Wow*.

I shook her gently. She opened one eye to squint at me. Then she rolled over, with her back toward me, and said, "*Go away!*"

I slipped my hand under the cover and pinched her bottom. She sat up with a squeal, laughing. It was going to be a wonderful day—or so I thought.

We sat together at the breakfast bar in my kitchen. She'd made pancakes. I'd made more coffee.

"What's up, Harry?" she asked. "You're very quiet. Can I help?"

Most women, when they ask that question, don't want to know the answer. Not so with Amanda. I'd known her less than a year, but she already knew almost as much about me as I knew myself. She could tell when I had something on my mind. Not only that, she was a newshound, an investigative reporter, and yes, she sure as hell *could* help.

"It's this Angela Hartwell thing Kate dumped in my lap," I told her. "I have a feeling it's going to get away from me. I thought at first it would be simple, a few questions, and then it would be done. But...." I reached for my jacket. I'd laid it over one of the bar stools when we came home the night before. I fished the list of questions out of my wallet and handed it to her. She unfolded it, read it, looked up at me, her eyes wide—then she read it again. Finally, she put it down and picked up her coffee.

"See what I mean?" I asked. "I have almost nothing."

She nodded. "What do you want me to do?"

Dumb as it sounds, I wasn't expecting that reaction, and I had to think about it.

"Well, you're a member of the club. You must have known her, and her husband Regis, right?"

"I did, but not well. They moved in different circles. He was a financier. Me? I'm just a working girl with my membership paid for by the Station, a perk with benefits, if you know what I mean."

I did.

"What *did* you know about them?"

She sat for a moment, sipping her coffee with both

hands wrapped around the mug, her eyes closed, her brow furrowed, thinking.

"She went to GPS, I think."

Girl's Preparatory School, or GPS, is an upscale high school for girls in Chattanooga. It costs the world to send your kid there, but it sets them up for a life of privilege.

"His folks were old money. Lived up on Stonehenge. They sent him and his younger brother, Ralph, to Baylor."

Hmmm, Baylor, huh?

Baylor is another upscale school in Chattanooga, and a rival to my own school, McCallie.

"They were bankers," she continued. "They owned a string of Hartwell Community Banks, maybe more than that, I don't really know. When his father died, Regis inherited everything. Ralph just got a trust fund. Regis sold the family home and moved to Mountain Shadows, and when he died the banks went to Ralph."

"I know most of the business stuff," I said. "Tim did some digging. What do you know about Ralph Hartwell?"

"I've never met him."

"I'm sensing a 'but.'"

"Well, there was a rumor going around just before Regis died that he was going to sell out to one of the big banks, and that Ralph tried to stop him—we covered the story—but... well, Regis died before the deal went through. That's about all I know. Regis and Angela were nice people, quiet, very discreet, enjoyed life, whatever."

"So if the sale of the banks had gone through, Ralph would have gotten nothing. Regis would have banked the cash from the sale and his bro would have been out in the cold, right?"

"That's about the size of it. As it is, Ralph now owns and runs the company, and Angela inherited only the personal assets—but those were substantial. I'd guess her net worth must be somewhere in the region of... eight, maybe ten million."

"Who gets that? Any idea?"

"They had no children, and her parents were killed in a car wreck when she was very young, so... the brother?"

"That's motive, Mandy. Real motive."

"Don't you ever call me that. I've told you before. I hate it."

I grinned at her. "I know. I was just pulling your chain."

"Well don't. It's not couth."

I grinned at her. "Okay, *Amanda*," I said. "So Ralph not only had a hell of a motive to kill Regis, he also had one to kill Angela. But unless she suspected him of her husband's death, why would he? He doesn't need the money, and to risk a second murder just to get his hands on a few million when he has hundreds of millions would just be stupid. Greed, maybe. That's always a prime mover. But that's a stretch. I need to talk to Ralph, and soon."

I looked at my watch. It was after ten. I needed a little time. Time to be quiet, to think. And then....

"Okay," I said. "Here's what I'd like to do...."

We dressed casually that morning. I was in a blue and white striped golf shirt, lightweight golf slacks, and

ECCO Golf Street shoes. Amanda, as always, was dressed to kill: a pale blue slip of a sun dress and matching Ferragamo sandals with three-inch heels.

We arrived at the club around eleven thirty. I'd called earlier and booked a table for lunch. I'd also called my father and asked him to join us. It was Saturday morning, and he had an early tee time, so he said he would. We were at my usual table in the bay window overlooking the ninth when he walked in.

"Hello Amanda, Harry," He looked at his watch. "Not late, am I?"

He wasn't late, and I said so. He sat down beside Amanda and waved at Doug, the bartender of the day, got his attention, then pointed to each of us and himself, indicating he wanted a round of drinks.

The place was busy. I should have known better than to expect to be able to talk, but the club seemed to be the place I needed to be. It was where we found the body, if not the place where Angela died, and all of her friends were members. Amanda and I were members too, but we didn't live there, as my father seemed to do. If there was anything or anybody worth knowing, he knew it.

The drinks came—a Blue Moon beer for me, no orange slice, a vodka tonic for Amanda, and a gin and tonic for my Old Man.

"Well, Harry," he said. "I know you've better things to do than eat lunch with your dear old dad. What do you need?"

"You make it sound like I never call you unless I need something, and that's just not true. You know that."

"That I do. But not this time. What's on your mind? I'll help if I can."

"Well, you know Kate dumped this Angela Hartwell thing in my lap. And—"

"Yes, of course," he interrupted. "And how is the lovely lieutenant? Haven't seen her in a while."

Jeez, he never had been very tactful. I glanced at Amanda. She wore an enigmatic smile.

"She's fine. Listen, Dad. Were you here on Wednesday evening between nine o'clock and midnight?"

"No. I was here until about nine and then I left. Why d'you ask?"

"Did you see Angela Hartwell?"

He thought for a moment. "I did. At about seven thirty, maybe eight. She was sitting over there, talking to Ed Gray."

"Ed Gray? You mean the cardiologist?"

"Yes. I was with Henry Strange and Larry, having a few drinks. She came in around... oh, seven thirty or so. He joined her a few minutes later. Come to think of it, I've seen them together several times. Never thought anything of it, though."

"Do you have any idea what they might have been talking about?"

"Good Lord, no. I may be a nosy lawyer, but I don't eavesdrop on private conversations. It was... serious, though, I think. Neither one of them looked very happy."

"Isn't Ed Gray married?" Amanda asked.

"Why yes." He looked at her. "I suppose he is."

"How well did you know her? Could they have been having an affair?" I asked.

"I didn't know her well. Just enough to say hello, in passing. I wouldn't know if they were having an affair. How would I?"

"Did they leave together?"

"That I don't know. I wasn't taking much notice of them. They could have, I suppose."

"What about Regis Hartwell. Did you know him?"

"Better than his wife. I had some dealings with him, bank business, and I played golf with him a couple of times. Other than that.... Well, I liked him?"

"If I wanted to get the inside information, who would I talk to?"

"Hmmm." He thought for a moment, then said, "I suppose Ben and Joan Loftis would be your best bet. They were close. Played golf and tennis together. Met here three, sometimes four times a week, and were always here for Sunday lunch. I know Ben well. Play with him two or three times a month. Nice fella. Haven't had much to do with Joan, but she seems nice enough. I'll introduce you, if you like."

"If you wouldn't mind. Are they here now?"

He looked around. "They're at the bar. Give me a minute. I'll go get them." And he did. He brought them over and made the introductions.

He was right about them being a nice couple. Both of them were about thirty-five. Average, well-to-do people with no edge about them.

I ordered drinks for everyone. I felt a little awkward,

not knowing them, and such a social setting was really not the place to conduct an interview, but what the hell. I plunged right in.

"I'm afraid I had an ulterior motive for wanting to meet you both. I hope you don't mind. I'm investigating the death of Angela Hartwell, and I understand you were good friends. Would you mind if I asked you a few questions?" I said it to Ben, who was seated to the left of my father, but I could tell I had taken them both by surprise.

"Well... yes, actually," Ben said. "Joan was one of Angela's best friends, but you're a private investigator. Aren't the police handling the investigation?"

"Yes, of course. I've been brought in as a consultant." I took out my wallet and gave him my card, and one of Kate's. "I understand your reluctance to talk to me, but if you would like to call Lieutenant Gazzara—her number is on the card—she'll explain the situation."

"No... no, no. There's no need for that. I know who you are, Mr. Starke. Hell, who around here doesn't?" He handed back Kate's card and pocketed mine. "You've built quite a reputation for yourself, second only to that of August, here. We'll be glad to help, won't we Joan."

"If it will help you get the bastard who killed Angela, yes of course," Joan said. It was a voice that could have cut diamonds. "Ask away."

Whew. I think I know who wears the pants in this family, I thought, then said, "Thank you, both of you. I appreciate it. If you don't mind, I'd like to record our conversation. Is that okay?"

They looked at each other. She shrugged, and he said, "Sure."

Amanda took a small digital recorder from her clutch and handed it to me. I turned it on, recorded the time, date, and those present, and then I hid it from prying eyes beside the floral centerpiece.

"Let's begin with last Wednesday evening," I said. "Angela was here. Were you also here?"

They both shook their heads.

"I need a verbal answer please," I said, smiling at them.

"Oh," Ben said. "Er... no. We were not here."

"She was seen between seven and eight o'clock with Dr. Ed Gray. Do either of you know him?"

"Yes, of course. He's also a good friend of ours."

"Would you have any idea what the two of them might have been doing here, alone together?"

"Not what you're thinking," Joan said angrily. "Ed is happily married, and Angela wasn't like that."

"Like what?"

"You know what I mean. She doesn't... didn't fool around. Ever."

"So what were they doing, do you think?"

"I have no doubt," Joan said, "that they were talking about Regis, and how he died. Ed is a cardiologist, you know."

"I did know, but why would they be talking about his death?"

"One," Ben said, "Regis died of a heart attack. Two, she made no secret of the fact that she thought he'd been murdered."

Oh boy. Here we go. I sat way back, leaning against the leather upholstery of the window seat.

"You're serious, right?" I said.

"Hell yes he's serious," Joan said, "and he's not alone. Regis was only thirty-eight, in peak physical condition. Mr. Starke, Regis Hartwell finished in the top 100 in the Boston Marathon three times."

I was stunned. "Did you know about this?" I asked, as I looked at my father.

"Oh, I'd heard rumors," he said, "but I discounted them. In my business you hear that kind of stuff all the time. There's never anything to it. And... well, she was very upset."

I looked at Joan and Ben. "Was there any other reason why she might have felt that her husband's death was unnatural?"

"Several," Joan said, a hard edge to her voice. "Regis thought someone was stealing money from his company. He was also determined to sell it, the company, the banks —that little skink Ralph, his brother, was having a conniption fit over it."

"Stealing? How? Who?"

"I don't know," she said. "They kept it quiet. Those kinds of rumors weren't good for the bank or the sale. I only knew because Angela told me."

I nodded. That's a new one. I wondered if it was true. If it was....

"Okay," I said. "Tell me about Ralph."

"There's not much to tell," she said. "He hated Regis, because their father left the company to him and not them both. Smart man, old Chester Hartwell. Knew his sons well. Ralph is a slimy little bastard. It wouldn't surprise me if it was him that was stealing from the company. Look, there's nothing more we can tell you," she said, getting to her feet. "We loved the Hartwells as though they were family. I loved Angela like a sister. You get whoever did this to her, please."

She turned away from the table and walked back into the bar. Ben wished us a subdued good afternoon, then followed her. We three sat looking after them.

"Well, now," August said brightly. "I think that calls for another drink, don't you?"

I did, and so did Amanda. He went to the bar to fetch them. I saw him talking for a moment to Ben Loftis, his hand on his shoulder. Sympathizing, I shouldn't wonder.

"What do you think, Harry?" Amanda asked.

"I think that maybe Angela was right, that Regis might well have been murdered. If so, this is not at all what I wanted. I don't have the resources to handle multiple murder investigations. Well, I guess I'll have to do what I can. Angela suffered a very nasty death, and someone is going to pay for it. I'll talk to Kate on Monday and see if I can get some help."

"Maybe I can help."

I looked at her, quizzically. "How?"

"Oh come on, Harry. I'm an investigative journalist. It's what I do, remember? I talk to people. Interview them. Ask questions. I'm a member here. I know just about everyone. I knew Angela, and I knew all of her friends—some of them not so well, granted, but I know who they are. I can help you. Yes?"

Damn. Why didn't I think of that? I nodded. "Yes. Let's do it. But first we need to think it through. And then

I need to talk to Ed Gray and Ralph. We'll talk more when we get home, okay?"

She gave me one of those smiles that sent shivers down my spine and said, "I don't think we'll be doing a whole lot of talking. Maybe tomorrow."

August brought the drinks and sat down.

"Are we going to eat?" he said.

"Yes, of course," Amanda answered. "I'm starving."

We ordered. I had a chicken Caesar salad, Amanda had a club sandwich, and dear old Dad had a small ribeye steak, rare, with red potatoes and asparagus. We ate, for the most part, in silence. My head was full of questions I had no answers to.

When we finished eating it was close to one thirty, and August said his goodbyes and left for the locker room, saying something about another nine holes.

"Sit down for a minute, Joe," I said to the waiter, when he came to see if we wanted more drinks.

"I can't, Mr. Starke. I'm working."

"Yeah, you can. The place is about empty. I'll square it with Doug. Sit."

He did.

"Were you working on Wednesday night?" I asked.

"Wednesday? Yes, I was here till they locked the doors. It was quiet, not much going on."

"Did you see Angela Hartwell?"

"Yes, she came in early, around five o'clock. Stayed for a few minutes and then left. She talked to Doug. She came back later, at around seven, I think it was. She left again sometime after eight. I really wasn't paying attention."

"While she was here the second time, she talked to Ed Gray, right?"

He nodded. "For maybe thirty minutes. I served drinks to them twice. She also had a few words with Ralph and Mary Hartwell. They were at the far end of the bar."

"Did you hear what they were talking about, her and Ed Gray, by chance?"

"I don't make a habit of listening in on member's conversations. It's not proper."

I smiled at him. It was an old-fashioned way of looking at things, but hey. It was nice to know some people have the right idea.

"They left about eight thirty, right?"

"She did. He left a few minutes after, maybe five minutes."

So, they could have met up again outside. "Now, Joe. This is important. Did she talk to anyone else while she was here?"

He thought for a minute, then said, "She said hello to several of the members. Exchanged pleasantries and so on. That's about it."

"Did you see her leave?"

"I did."

"Was she alone? Did anyone follow her?"

"She was alone, and no I didn't see anyone follow her."

"Okay. Thanks, Joe. I appreciate it." I handed him my card. "If you think of anything, please call me." He said he would, then went back to his duties. He got about halfway to the bar then hesitated, and seemed about to turn, but didn't.

I rose and followed him to the bar.

"Joe," I said. "It seemed to me that you might have thought of something. What was it?"

He shook his head, "Nothing really. I just remembered that when Mrs. Hartwell was walking out into the lobby, I saw her stop and exchange a few words with Ms. Archer."

"Ruth Archer?"

"Yes sir."

"Did they talk for long? Were they friendly with each other, angry, what?"

"I'd say friendly, from what I could see—which wasn't much. Mrs. Hartwell had her back to me. Ms. Archer was smiling."

I nodded, thanked him, and returned to the table.

"Anything?" Amanda asked.

"No. Not really. She bumped into Ruth Archer on the way is all."

"I don't like that woman."

I smiled at her. "Of course you don't." She let it go.

Well," she said. "I don't know about you, but I know less now than when we arrived. What was she doing with Ed Gray, I wonder?"

"There's only one way to find out. I need to talk to him, and to Ralph. Wouldn't hurt to have a word with Doug, the bartender, either."

We stopped by the bar on the way out. He was cleaning up.

"Hey, Doug," I said.

"Hello, Mr. Starke. What can I do for you? More drinks?"

"No, thanks. I have a question, if you don't mind."

"About Angela Hartwell? Joe said you talked to him."

"About her, yeah. Joe tells me she stopped by around five o'clock on Wednesday, and that she spoke to you. Do you mind telling me what the conversation was about?"

"It wasn't a conversation. She was looking for Dr. Gray. I told her I hadn't seen him. She said she'd be back later, and then she left. That's it."

I nodded, thanked him, and then we left, too.

8

I hadn't been at my desk more than ten minutes that Monday morning when my iPhone rang. I looked at the screen. I didn't recognize the number.

"Harry Starke," I said.

"Hello, Mr. Starke. This is Ruth Archer. Do you have a minute?"

Ruth Archer. Wow. I pictured the woman I'd met at the club just a few days ago. The goddess.

"What can I do for you, Ms. Archer?"

"I'm not really sure. I have a bit of a problem. I think I'm being stalked." *Oh yeah?*

"What makes you think that?"

"Oh, it's just a feeling. It may be nothing, but... well, you know."

Yeah, I did know. "Tell you what. If you give me your address, I'll send someone over to talk to you."

"Oh no. That won't do at all. I want to talk to *you*. Look. I'm at the club. I was going to play. Why don't you join me? We can talk on the course."

And there it was. I should have seen it coming. What the hell was she after? "I can't, sorry. I'm swamped. It will have to be one of my investigators, or... well, that's what it'll have to be."

"Not good enough, Mr. Starke. Suppose the same thing happens to me that happened to Angela Hartwell. How would you feel then, knowing you might have been able to stop it?"

Well, she had me there. It was bullshit, and I knew it, but what if.... Well, you get the picture. I had to find out what she was up to, and there was only one way to do that.

"Okay. I'll be there in forty-five minutes, just to talk. Nothing more.

She wasn't in the bar when I arrived, so I took a seat at an empty table to wait. It was only for a couple of minutes.

She was dressed for golf. She was wearing what I thought might be a skort. You know, it looks like a very short skirt, but they have shorts underneath. But when she came closer I saw that she was not wearing a skort. It was a pink tennis skirt, and it left little to the imagination. Everything else was pink too: socks, shoes, visor—everything but her shirt, and even the lining on that was pink. *Who the hell does she think she is, Paula Creamer?*

Paula Creamer is one of the goddesses of the LPGA Tour, but this woman would have put Paula in the shade. She was almost as tall as me, had a figure half a million bucks couldn't buy, and her legs? They were tanned, muscled, and... long.

She flopped down on the seat opposite, exposing

every inch of those legs to me. They were everywhere. Tall as she was, she had a job keeping them to herself, not that I was complaining.

Good job Amanda isn't here.

"Good morning, Harry," she said. "It's so good of you to come out here at such short notice. Thank you."

I nodded. "What is it you want, Ms. Archer?"

"Two things. One, I want to talk to you about my stalker. Second... I want to play with you. Golf, of course," she said with a smile, when she saw the look on my face.

"That's not going to happen."

"Oh but it is. I'm going to make it worth your while. I'll pay you for your time, and we'll talk as we play. How much do you charge for your time, Harry?"

"I charge $350 an hour, but I don't have time. So forget it." I actually charge $175 per hour, but what the hell.

"Eighteen holes, say three hours. That would be $1,000, give or take. I'll pay you $2,000 for the three hours. Come on. What do you say? It will be fun."

What the hell is she up to? Only one way to find out. "Okay," I said, "but no fee. We'll play. You'll talk. That's it."

"Fine. Go get changed. I can't wait."

Hell, now neither can I.

I called Jacque and told her to hold down the fort, that I would be back after lunch, and then I went to the locker room to change. I was already wearing the clothes for golf; all I had to do was change shoes and have the attendant take my clubs out to where she was waiting with the cart.

"You want to loosen up a little?" she asked.

I shook my head and got behind the wheel of the cart. Her clubs—pink bag, of course—and mine, were already strapped to the rear. We drove out to the first tee.

"So," she said, when we stepped onto the tee. "What would you like to play for?"

"Stakes, do you mean? I thought this was to be a friendly game and a chat."

"That, too," she said, "but let's make it interesting. You name it."

"Look, lady, I'm not stupid. You have a two handicap; I have a nine. No, let's keep it friendly."

She laughed. "You're right, of course. Tell you what. I'll play off the men's tees; the same ones you play off, and I'll give you... five shots. How's that?"

How's that? You're a hustler. That's how's that. I sighed. "Okay, $100. Match play."

That opened her eyes wide. "*Match play*. How unique. I like it. But $100? No. I tell you what. Let's do it this way. If you win, I'll give you $100. If I win...." There was a twinkle in her eye that I didn't like. "You buy me dinner."

I looked at her. Amanda would have my guts if I went for it.

"No," she said in a low voice. "I don't believe it. The great Harry Starke is scared of losing. Who would have thought it?" That did it. *Sorry, Amanda.*

"Okay," I said. "You take the honor."

She did.

The first was a par four, 436 yards to an elevated green. The landing area off the tee was generous, easy to hit, and, for a low handicapper, a good long drive would leave an easy four or five iron to the green. For me it was a good long drive and then a three hybrid, if I got lucky.

The ladies' tee is set some 100 yards farther forward of the men's tees, but that's not where she was. She was with me, on the big boy tee box. I watched as she bent down and teed her ball. I wanted to look away, but I couldn't. She definitely wasn't wearing a skort.

She stepped away from the ball, driver in hand, and stood behind it to get her line. Then she stepped back to the ball and addressed it. Her swing was one of the most beautiful I'd seen outside of the PGA tour, and she hammered her ball a solid 300 yards right down the middle, leaving herself maybe a nine iron into the green.

Oh hell, Harry. You are in some kind of trouble.

She bent over, picked up her tee, turned, looked at me, then smiled with her head cocked to one side.

Well, I did my best, but my best was thirty yards short of hers. I had roughly 155 yards to the flag. It would take as good of a seven-iron shot as I'd ever hit to have any chance.

I pulled the seven from my bag. She sat in the cart, watching. I could feel her eyes boring into my back as I addressed the ball. Yep, I was intimidated.

I hit that ball as good as I ever had. I watched as it soared up and onward and then down onto the green. *Eat that one, Missy.*

"Nice one, Harry. Well done." She clapped as I climbed back into the cart and drove to her ball.

She pulled a pitching wedge from her bag, not even bothering to get her line before proceeding to fly the ball right to the center of the green, taking a divot that must have been all of two feet long in the process. She bent over to pick up the divot, making sure I had a good view of her ass. I watched her as she replaced it. Golf wasn't the only game she was playing.

We drove to the green. The two balls were within ten feet of the hole; hers was maybe a foot closer than mine, which meant I had to putt first. My nerves were jangling. Nevertheless, I managed to lip the ball into the hole for a birdie three. I had never birdied the first hole in my life. This was a first I felt a thrill run through me. I looked at her. *Game on, girl.*

Unfortunately, she made her putt and birdied it, too. *Oh what fun.*

By the time we reached the seventh tee, she was two up, and I was feeling like a damp rag. She was playing like a pro, and I was playing like the amateur that I was. Fortunately, she was giving me five shots, the first of them coming on this, the par five seventh, where we'd found Angela Hartwell in the river beside the green.

"Isn't this where you found Angela's body?" she asked.

"Yes, just over there, in the shallow water just to the left of the green." I nodded in the general direction.

"I don't know how you do it," she said.

"Do what?"

"Deal with all those dead bodies. It must be absolutely horrible."

"You can say that again," I said, as I took my three

iron from the bag. "Your honor." I watched as she teed her ball. I shook my head in wonder. *How come some people are blessed not only with great beauty, but also great talent? This one has it all. I bet she can sing, too.*

She stepped back behind the ball, crouching down to get her line, then she straightened, looked at me, smiled, and walked around and addressed the ball.

Jeez, will you look at that. No wonder I'm getting beat. She's making my head ache.

And then I noticed that, not only was she beating me off the men's tees, she was also playing with men's clubs.

Damn!

Her swing was a long, loping loop; her hips turned to the left and her back arched; the club head finished close to her heels. It was a thing of beauty. The ball lifted on the spin, dropping to the center of the fairway some 270 yards out, and rolled on for 20 more. I shook my head. I was doomed to take this beauty to dinner. Amanda would be outraged.

I took my usual three iron. There was no point in trying to hit a driver. I just wasn't that good. I hit a good shot to the center of the fairway, maybe 220 yards. She had me by at least sixty yards. The only consolation was that I was there in zero, because of my free shot, while she was where she was in one.

Down on the fairway, I took out my five wood—they call them metals these days—and I hit a good shot to within 160 yards of the flag. I was there in one. If I could get up and down, I'd have a natural birdie. With my shot, it would be an eagle; I'd be only one down. With four more shots I'd be in with a chance.

We drove to her ball, where she did the whole bend and straighten routine again, then hammered the ball with a three iron to within 100 yards of the green. The woman was on fire. I had to do something

I stood over my ball, thought about it, shook my head. It wasn't a difficult shot, but with the goddess watching, and a dinner that would get me into more trouble than I could handle on the line....

I sighed, dragged out my seven iron, tried to relax, and then.... I watched the ball as it gained altitude. It was bang on line, and then it dropped down onto the green, out of sight. I knew it was good, but how good?

"Very nice, Harry. I'm beginning to get the idea that you don't want to buy me dinner."

I didn't answer. I just smiled at her.

She took a pitching wedge and, with an easy sweep, lofted the ball onto the green. It wasn't as good a shot as mine, I could tell, but still.

When we got to where we could see the surface of the green, I couldn't help it, I laughed. My ball—I just knew it was mine—was within two feet of the hole. Hers was at least twenty feet away.

"Damn you, Harry Starke." She said it with a smile, and without malice. She putted the ball to within three feet, then sank it for a par five. I was lying net two. I sank the putt for a net eagle. We were all square, and I still had four shots coming to me.

YES!

"So, Harry," she said. "Show me where you found poor Angela." I did. I walked her down to the riverbank and we stood there in silence. What she was thinking about, I had no idea. I did know what I was thinking about, and it wasn't pleasant.

"So, do you have any suspects yet?" She asked, thoughtfully.

"No."

"How is the investigation going?"

"Right now, it isn't. It's still very early."

"What about that forty-eight hours thing? Don't you need to have it solved by then?"

"That would have been nice, but that's rarely what happens, especially in a case like this one."

"Where are you focusing your efforts?

I looked at her. *What the hell?*

"I'm asking questions. It's how you get the answers," I said, with no little sarcasm. She didn't seem to notice.

"Do you think this is where she died?"

"I don't know. Could be. Could be she died elsewhere and was dumped here."

"And you have no persons of interest at all?"

"Why are you asking all these questions? Do you know something?"

"Nope, just curious. It's very interesting. Come on. Let's play golf. I'm looking forward to our dinner together."

The hell you say!

The game was close. It all came down to the eighteenth hole. We stood on the tee all square, thanks to my having received three more shots, and I still had one for the final hole. I had a chance.

But when she hit her third to within eight feet of the hole, I was in trouble. I was on the green in four, net three, thanks to my free shot—I'd managed to find the fairway bunker midway out, and that had cost me one. Now, as I said, I was lying net three some thirty feet from the pin with a break to the left of at least three feet staring up at me. If I missed, and she made hers, dinner was on me. Somehow, though, I wasn't worried. *It is what it is.*

I got behind the ball and figured out what I hoped would be the line. I addressed the ball, swung the putter smoothly on through, watching as the ball rolled interminably and... inevitably into the hole. I stood there, stunned, and so did Ruth Archer—and up on the terrace overlooking the green, so did Amanda. If Ruth missed her eight-footer now, she would owe me $100. She didn't.

"Well damn," she said, walking up and shaking my hand. "I guess I'll just have to figure out another way to get you all to myself." And with that she walked off the green into the clubhouse, her hips swinging, leaving me to see to the cart and clubs.

Ten minutes later, I was seated in the bar with Amanda drinking a double gin and tonic, and I needed it.

"You, Harry Starke," she said, "are one lucky S.O.B. She had you there. And if you'd have had to take her to dinner... well, let's not talk about it."

"Lucky my ass. I just played my best round of golf in three years, maybe more. I shot a two over seventy-four. She was two under, for God's sake. And I had a plan anyway. Yes, I would have had to buy her dinner, but nothing was said about it being just her...."

"You sneaky...."

"Yeah, yeah, yeah. But listen. I'm thinking she has some kind of an agenda...."

"Hah, and we all know what that is."

"No, Amanda. That's not what I meant. I think she might have been on a fishing expedition. She asked an awful lot of questions, about Angela Hartwell and the investigation. I asked her why. She said she was just curious, but... well, there was something, and for the life of me I can't figure out what it could be, unless.... Who knows? Something to think about, though."

"Well, like I told you before, she's as crooked as a bent nail."

I nodded. "Her excuse for wanting to meet with me today was that she thought she was being stalked but she never even mentioned it, and I forgot to ask her. I was too focused on not losing the match."

"Yes, good job, too." She was smiling, but not with her eyes, and I knew I had to change the subject.

"Right. Let's get some lunch and then get out of here," I said. "Are you working today?"

"Yes, I have to do the six and eleven o'clock news. Why?"

"Can you get someone to cover for you?"

"I suppose, but why?"

"Just being selfish. I need a quiet evening. Time to think. I thought maybe you'd like it if I cooked dinner."

"You sneaky...." She took her iPhone from her clutch, hit the speed dial, talked for a few moments, disconnected, looked at me, then smiled and nodded.

CHAPTER9

I called Jacque and told her I was taking the rest of the day off, and that I'd be in bright and early the following morning. It didn't go down well.

Next, I called Kate and told her the same—that turned into a much longer conversation, but her overall reaction was the same as Jacque's, though I told her I would call her in the morning and bring her up to speed.

I must admit, I had a small twinge of conscience about taking the time off, but what the hell. That's why I run my own company. I make the rules. Besides, I wasn't really taking time off; I just needed the rest of the afternoon to think about the case, do a little organizing. I could have done all that at my office, but there it would be one interruption, one distraction after another. Better I do it at home, where I wouldn't be disturbed. That was what I told myself.

The calls made, I returned to the bar. Amanda had ordered a second round of drinks, which was... well, not good, but again, what the hell?

It was still early, a little after two o'clock, when we got to my house. I'd already had more to drink than I should, so I made coffee—but not with the Keurig.

I love coffee and, over the years, have become something of a connoisseur. I've tried most of the expensive brands, even Kopi Luwak, which is the one that's eaten by and fermented inside a little animal called the civet. I tried it because I felt I had to, and it was very good, but I just couldn't get the image of... well, you know. Couldn't get that out of my head. Anyway, I felt like a treat, so I liberated one of my bags of Jamaican Blue Mountain from its air-tight container, put the water on to heat, and prepared the French press: eight level teaspoons of coffee made four eight-ounce cups, two for each of us. I drink it with a teaspoon full of half-and-half, no sugar, and let me tell you, it's exquisite.

I handed a cup to Amanda, and we retired to the sofa in front of the great windows. She was about to speak, but I put a hand on her arm. When I drink Blue Mountain, that's all I want to do: sit quietly and enjoy the moment.

After we'd each consumed our second cup, she said finally, "Okay, Mr. Coffee. What was that all about?"

I looked at her, bemused. "Amanda. You've just experienced something wonderful, something very few folks ever get to enjoy, and you wonder what it was all about? Didn't you like it?"

She screwed up her face, "I suppose. It was okay."

"*Okay*? Just okay? You just guzzled down twenty bucks worth of the best coffee in the world and it was just okay?"

She burst out laughing, "Oh Harry, you're such a chump sometimes. Coffee is coffee. How different can it be? I liked it. It was okay."

"Wow. No more of the good stuff for you, then. From now on you can drink the supermarket crap. Remind me to get some in for you."

Okay my ass.

"Time to go to work," I said, getting up from the sofa. "We've lots to sort out, so let's get on with it."

"Hey, no, we've plenty of time. Come back and sit with me for a minute."

"No ma'am. I get back down there with you, I'll never get up again. I came home to work, and work I will, with or without you."

She pouted.

Damn. I *almost* gave in.

"Later." I said. "Now, we work."

I went into the cubicle I called my office—it was actually a large walk-in closet, but I'd had to give up the spare bedroom the day Amanda started moving her stuff in. She didn't live with me, but only technically. I think she had more clothes at my place than she did at home, and she spent more time here than there, too.

I grabbed a couple of legal pads and some colored pens, cleared the dining table, and sat down. Amanda was at the window, looking out over the river. The light shone through her flimsy summer dress. She was bewitching. The longer I watched her, the more my will deteriorated. I walked over to stand behind her, slipped my arms around her waist and nuzzled her ear.

"That's not fair," I whispered in her ear.

"No, it's not." She turned, wrapped her arms around my neck, and kissed me.

I let it happen, but pushed her gently away before things could go any further. "Later. Right now I have to work.

She smiled. "I'm holding you to that first part."

I sat back down at the table. She also sat, opposite me. We talked back and forth, making notes and spreading sheets of paper all over the table until well after five, by which time my head was spinning, and so, I think, was hers. During the past three hours I'd consumed five cups of coffee, and I was wired; Amanda had switched to Riesling right around three o'clock and was already on her third glass when I decided to categorize and prioritize everything we'd gone through before calling it a day.

My subject list had grown to almost two dozen pages, of which several stood out.

I needed to know more about Regis Hartwell, his life and death, his friends, his business, and whether or not someone really was stealing from his banks.

I needed to know a lot more about Angela Hartwell, too. Someone needed her to die. Why? What was she doing, or what did she know, that was so threatening? Someone had searched her apartment. What were they looking for? What was she doing and who was she with during those two hours after she left the club, before she met her end?

Dr. Ed Gray might be able to answer at least some of those questions, so that would be first on my list of things to do.

Motive was my next concern. Who benefitted from Angela's death? Only one person that I could think of: Ralph Hartwell. But he might not be the only one. If someone had been stealing, and Angela knew about it, or if they even suspected she knew about it... that opened up the field to all sorts of people—people I didn't even know. I had to find out more, and Ed Grey might, again, be able to point me in the right direction. In the meantime....

I grabbed my iPhone and punched in the number for Tim's direct line. He answered immediately.

"Hey, Tim," I said. "It's me. I need you to do me a favor. Angela Hartwell's cell phone is missing. Can you see if you can find it? You can tell me what you find when I get in tomorrow morning. Seven thirty."

I gave him the number of the missing phone, and he said he'd get right on it. Then I asked him to put me through to Ronnie.

Ronnie Hall is one of my staff. With a background in banking and an MSc in finance from the London School of Economics, he handles my white-collar investigations.

He didn't answer the phone, so I left a message.

"Hey Ronnie. I have a question that's been bugging me for a couple of days. How does someone steal from a bank without actually walking in and holding it up at gunpoint? I don't need to know right now, but if you could give me something in the morning, that would be great. Talk to you then. Bye."

That done, I felt a little more relaxed. Tomorrow morning I'd have answers to some of my tech questions. Now I had to go see the people I hoped could fill in the gaps.

Two more calls later I had an appointment with Ed Gray for ten-thirty the next day, and one for noon with Ralph Hartwell.

Next, I called Kate and told her I needed her present for both meetings. She agreed to meet me at my office as soon as she could tear herself free.

Finally, I put Amanda to digging through the Channel 7 archives—no, not that evening, in the morning. I wanted anything and everything to do with Hartwell Community Banks, and I knew that if it was there, she would find it. After that I really did feel better.

It was almost six o'clock by the time I finished. I was bushed, and so was Amanda. We called it a day.

"So," she said, a large glass of white wine in hand, "What are you going to feed me?"

Damn. I'd completely forgotten I'd promised to cook.

"I dunno. To be honest, I haven't given it a whole lot of thought. Scrambled eggs and toast, maybe?" I asked hopefully.

"Ugh, you really know how to show a girl a good time. I was thinking more along the lines of poached salmon with asparagus."

Poached salmon and asparagus? I had 'em both, but damn. I really didn't want to cook.

I looked at her. She was laughing.

"It's okay, scrambled eggs will be fine...."

"Wait," I said. "I have an idea." I hit the app on my iPhone, found what I was looking for, smiled at her, and went into the bedroom to order. An hour later, Dinner Delivered showed up at the door with... yep, you guessed it: salmon filet with asparagus for Amanda and a sixteen ounce T-bone with fries for me.

And it was great, too. Not quite up to my own standards, but close enough. Needless to say, the evening turned out far better than I had expected an hour ago.

9

I'd told Tim I would be in the office by seven thirty that next morning, and I was. I spent the first thirty minutes in my cave with Jacque, making a list of things I needed to get done. We were just finishing up when Kate arrived. As always, she looked amazing, and it wasn't what she was wearing: just a simple white, sleeveless top, black pants, and loafers.

Jacque left, and I took the next several few minutes to bring Kate up to speed. She listened, made notes on her iPad, sipped her coffee, said little.

"What's wrong, Kate? You seem preoccupied."

She sighed. Then tilted her head back to look at the ceiling.

"You're right. I'm trying to run four murder investigations as well as this one. And this one looks to be turning into a bear. I hope you're wrong, but if Regis Hartwell *was* murdered, I'm going to have to get more involved. He was kinda prominent in this town—and a close friend of the mayor, too. He'll be all over it. You sure he was murdered?"

"No, but his wife was, and I don't believe in coincidence. Neither do you."

She nodded, took a deep breath. "I need more coffee. What else do you have?"

"Did CSI find anything at Angela's apartment?"

"I don't have that report yet. Apparently the place was a hell of a mess. We can follow up on that after the interviews."

"Okay. I gave Tim and Ronnie a couple of tasks yesterday; I need to see what they found, but it shouldn't take long. You can wait for a minute, right?"

I picked up the phone and asked Jacque to send in Tim and Ronnie, and also asked her to join us and take notes.

"Okay, people. I'm on a tight schedule this morning, so let's get started. Tim. Have you been able to find Angela Hartwell's cell phone?"

"Sorry, Mr. Starke. I can't find it. Either the battery's dead or it's been removed. It might even be at the bottom of the river where you found her."

"That's a thought," I said. "Kate would it be possible to organize a couple of divers from Wildlife Resources?"

"I'll see what I can do."

"What else do you have for me, Tim?"

"As I mentioned on Friday, she has an almost perfect credit score. 832. Her net worth is still a bit iffy, but I've managed to put a rough estimate together. She's worth—and this is a conservative estimate—$57.72 million."

"Are you kidding me?" I was astounded. "She was

twenty-nine years old, for Christ's sake. How the hell did that happen?"

"Well, it was easy enough since she inherited all of her husband's cash, real property, and investments. It seems he was a bit of a wiz with those, but I'll get to him in a minute. Mrs. Hartwell owned her home. Zillow estimates it to be worth $850,000, but I think that's a little on the low side. It's probably worth closer to a million. She also owned, and it's part of the net worth I already mentioned, a substantial amount of real property, including a hotel and a strip mall. Their investments in blue chip stocks are also substantial. She lived, as we know, in a rented apartment. There's almost $63,000 in one checking account and a little over $94,000 in another, and then there's $250,000 in liquid capital in a savings account. It would have been very easy to get her hands on money if she needed it. She was solid, Mr. Starke. That's about it. She was also a very private lady."

I shook my head. I'd known her, not well, and I'd known him slightly, but I never would have thought they were worth that kind of money. She certainly didn't dress the part. I looked at Tim and nodded for him to continue.

"She was an only child, and her parents are both dead, so, according to the way Regis set up the family trust, it all passes to his younger brother."

"Fifty-seven million good reasons to kill her, or have her killed," I said.

Tim nodded. "Regis Hartwell, as you know, died of a heart attack just over a year ago. He owned and operated the nine Hartwell Community Banks. When Mr. Hartwell passed, the Hartwell company passed to Ralph.

That business is estimated to be worth close to $900 million, including the bank buildings and liquid assets of more than 600 million."

He flipped through several screens on his iPad. "Ralph Hartwell was a year younger than Regis. Now he's thirty-eight and married to Mary, his second wife. No kids with her, but two from the previous marriage. He lives on Signal Mountain, and...." He looked up and around the table with a grin. "This is where it gets interesting. He was in deep financial trouble when his brother died. He was behind on his child support, credit card bills, car payments; he was two payments in arrears on his mortgage. He likes to live high off the hog. The first thing he did when he took over the banks was pay off his debts and raise his salary. His brother's death was—well, fortuitous?"

He paused to take a sip from his bottle of water. "His wife... uh, Mary, is a big spender. Drives a Mercedes, shops at Bergdorf, Neiman, you get the idea. Mary was his secretary at the main branch before they were married, and is probably the reason for the breakup of Ralph's first marriage. Oh, and they're both members of the country club."

"They are? Huh. How come I haven't run into them?" I looked at my watch. We were out of time. "That it, Tim?" He nodded.

"Good job, as always," I said. "And thank you. Jacque, could you get all that entered into the computer and break it down into short bites, please?

She nodded, and left the room. I turned and looked at

Ronnie. "Okay, smartass. How's it done? How do I rob a bank without setting foot inside?"

He grinned at me. "There are a number of ways, some of which Tim could help you with better than me, the Internet, hacking, etc., but he'll also tell you that it's become very difficult to hit the big banks directly. Their security is unbelievably complex, but the smaller banks are easier—community banks and savings and loan companies. But it's even easier to go for the bank's customers. A phishing expedition would gather the necessary personal information: account numbers, login, and so on. Not easy, but it can be done.

"The other way is relatively simple," Ronnie continued, "but much more labor intensive. It involves counterfeit checks on corporate accounts. They wouldn't actually be robbing the bank, per se, but the bank, if it wanted to retain its good name and reputation, would have to make good on the losses, so, technically...."

"How would that work?" I asked.

"Well, like I said, it's labor intensive, but if carried out by a dedicated team of crooks, it could produce significant results. The idea is to pick a mid-size company. A manufacturing company would probably be best, but not essential. What you do is get hold of one of their checks, make a dozen or so counterfeit copies, keeping the company name, routing number, and account number intact. You then write a counterfeit check to a bogus company for a small amount, less than $1,000 - say for materials or services rendered - deposit it in a bank account set up in the name of that phony company, and then you sit back and wait. If the check clears without problems or query, you're golden. You write a second check for a larger sum, say three or four thousand. The idea is to get the bank used to seeing the checks and the name. If that one goes through, you do it one more time. This time for fifteen or twenty thousand. You space the three or four checks out over a month, and then you quit while you're ahead. It takes that long for the target company's bookkeeping to catch up. So the third check has to go through before they can catch it. Then you clean the money out of the account, close it, and launder the money."

"But don't banks have safeguards in place to catch that kind of thing?" Kate asked. "It can't be that easy, surely."

"*Big* banks do. Small banks, community banks, and company savings and loans usually don't have that kind of sophistication. They can't afford it. Oh some do, but...."

"It can't be that easy," I said.

Ronnie just looked at me, an enigmatic smile on his face.

"Okay, so what you're saying is this: I steal a check, copy it, and write checks to myself, or some phony company I made up?"

"It's a bit more complicated than that, but essentially... yes."

"Where the hell would someone get a company check?" Kate asked.

"That's actually the most difficult part. The counterfeits have to look like the real thing."

"Come on, Ronnie. We're talking small potatoes here. Twenty or twenty-five thousand dollars is not worth killing for, nor can I see anyone making the effort." I said, skeptically.

"So you say," he replied. "But think about it this way: Eight or ten deals like that a month, and you're looking at some serious money, maybe as much as a quarter million. Repeat it five or six times a year, and that's several million dollars. Easy money. You hit each company once, then wait a year or so and hit them all again. Over two or three years... five, maybe as much as eight million."

He was right. I could see it. What I couldn't see was the kind of organization and dedication it would take to pull off such a heist on such a grand scale.

"Sorry, Ronnie," I said. "I just don't see it. You're talking a lot of companies, and a lot of banks. I don't think it's viable."

He shrugged. "It is if you have the resources. There are hundreds of companies within a hundred miles of Chattanooga, especially since VW and Amazon arrived. It could be done. And, I might add, it already *has* been done elsewhere. How do you think I came up with it?"

He had me there.

"Didn't you tell me that Joan Loftis said Regis Hartwell thought someone was stealing from his banks?" Kate asked. "Maybe they were."

I nodded. The more I thought about it, the more viable it became. Hartwell was operating nine bank branches. It was a perfect setup for what Ronnie had just described. And then I had a thought: *Especially if....*

"Okay, people. Good job. I need to get out of here. I have several appointments this morning." With that, I waited until they'd gone, all except Kate, and then I called Amanda. At the same time, Kate was calling to request divers be dispatched to the country club to try to find the phone.

"Hey, you," I said when Amanda picked up. "Listen, I know you're busy, but I was wondering if you'd found anything.... Yes, yes, yes... I know. I know you said you'd call if you had anything, but I just thought I'd—Okay. Call me later. Bye." *Jeez, I only asked.*

I looked at Kate. She was smiling, "All not well in paradise?" she asked.

I shrugged, "Amanda offered to help. She's digging through Channel 7's archives. Hell, Kate. I'm just as slammed as you are. I needed the help, and she offered. It's as simple as that."

"Methinks he doth protest too much." She grabbed her iPad from the coffee table. "Come on. Let's go. I don't have all day."

So we headed out to see Dr. Gray. On the way out, I told Jacque I'd be back sometime that afternoon.

Hah.

10

I'd arranged to meet Dr. Gray at his office at CHI Memorial Hospital—the Chattanooga Heart Institute. It was just a fifteen-minute drive from my office. I knew we wouldn't have a whole lot of time, though, since the doctor was sure to be busy.

Sure enough, the place was a bustling mass of humanity. CHI Memorial is always busy. He guided us along the maze of corridors back to his office, and we got to see it all.

Dr. Gray was a tall man, dressed in the obligatory white lab coat. He was perhaps a couple of years older than me—say forty-four or five—light red hair, clean shaven, slightly stooped, hands in the pockets of his coat, a bright smile on his face

"So you're Harry Starke," he said, sitting down behind his desk. His voice was much deeper than I'd expected. "I've heard a lot about you. I don't know whether to be impressed or frightened. Impressed, I think. And the lady is...?"

"Lieutenant Catherine Gazzara, Chattanooga PD, Doctor," Kate said, offering her hand. He rose from his seat, leaning over the desk to shake it. "I'm actually running the investigation. Mr. Starke is consulting."

"You said on the phone that you wanted to talk to me about Angela Hartwell." He looked at me as he said it. "Very well, what can I do for you?"

"Harry?" Kate prodded me.

"I know you must be busy, Doctor, so I'll get right to it. I understand you were with Angela Hartwell at the country club the night she died."

"Yes, we had a couple of drinks, talked for a while, and then she left. At about nine-thirty, I think."

"How was she? Upset? Worried? Did she seem to have anything on her mind?"

"As far as I could tell, she was perfectly normal. A bit harassed, intense, and yes, she had a lot on her mind, but that's the way she was."

"May I ask what you talked about?"

He sighed, shook his head, then said, "I was a good friend of Regis', which is how I knew Angela. How she knew me. Regis and I played together several times a week, mostly on the weekends. It came as a great shock to me when he died. Most unexpected, so it was. Picture of health, the man was...." He sat for a moment, staring down at his desk, seemingly lost in thought. After a while, he looked up again.

"Angela was convinced Regis was murdered. That was what we were talking about. That's what we always talked about. All Angela ever wanted to talk about."

"What made her think he was murdered?" I asked.

"Just that he was disgustingly healthy. To my knowledge, he hadn't seen a doctor in ten years. He was a runner, you know. Made the top 100 in the Boston Marathon several times. Sudden death happens, especially where the heart is concerned, but Regis.... Well. She ordered a post-mortem. Nothing. No signs of heart disease. It just stopped. She never got over it, poor girl."

"And what do *you* think? Could he have been murdered?"

"Sheesh." He pulled a face and sucked air in through his teeth. "Could have been, I suppose, though how, I have no idea. Who... well, Angela was convinced that her brother-in-law had something to do with it, but the tox screen revealed nothing. He'd had a drink, so there was a small amount of alcohol, but that was all."

I made a mental note of his reference to Ralph Hartwell, and continued.

"What about Potassium Chloride or SUX?"

"Succinylcholine chloride? I doubt it. It's almost impossible to obtain outside of a hospital, and highly regulated. Potassium Chloride... possibly. It would have to be injected, but there were no injection sites found during the post mortem, and Regis wouldn't have allowed anything like... that... unless...."

He stopped talking, stared down at his desktop again, his eyes closed.

"Unless what?" Kate asked.

"Unless he was drugged first. Damn, why didn't I think of that before? Any one of the date rape drugs would have rendered him non-resistant, then it would be easy enough to administer an injection. Potassium chloride would do it. He'd be dead in minutes."

"But you said no injection sites were found, and wouldn't the drugs that sedated him have shown up on the tox screen?" Kate asked.

"No, there are no tests for the so-called date rape drugs. GHB can be detected in the hair, but no one would think to look for it, and the others—Rohypnol, Ketamine and so on—no. Potassium chloride? The human body produces it naturally, so unless the levels were off the charts, it wouldn't be noticed. And an injection site probably wouldn't have been noticed if it was between the toes, or even in a nice vein in the ankle. One of the great myths of injecting is that it leaves a mark, and for multiple injections, that's true. But for a one-off, probably not. Needles these days are extremely fine, smaller even than a sewing needle, and will often leave no mark at all."

"So it could have been done, then?" I asked. "He could have been killed with Potassium chloride?"

"It's possible."

"But isn't the injectable type also hard to get?" Kate asked.

"Not so much. Vets use it all the time, and their offices get broken into rather regularly. There was a string of break-ins only last year, if you remember, here and in Cleveland."

Kate nodded thoughtfully.

"Look," he said, glancing at his watch. "I don't want to rush you, but...."

"Of course," I said. Just a few more questions, if you

don't mind. Doctor, why did Angela Hartwell think that her brother-in-law might have had something to do with Regis's death?"

"Regis and Ralph didn't get along. I know that from talking to Regis. He would have fired him if he could, but his father had set it up so that he couldn't. Smart man, old man Hartwell. Anyway, Regis was convinced Ralph was stealing from the company. He didn't have any proof—at least, if he did, he didn't tell me. But he was convinced Ralph was stealing, and I guess that if he could have proved it he would have, and Ralph would have gone to jail. Angela knew everything Regis knew, plus she's been digging around ever since Regis died. She told me she *did* have proof, but she didn't say what. That's all I know."

I nodded. "When she left you. Where was she going, did she say?"

"She said she was going home. That's it. Look, I'm sorry, I really do have to go. If you need to talk to me again, I'll be at the club tomorrow evening, after six, and on Saturday morning for my usual foursome. We have an early tee time and are usually off the course by eleven-thirty."

"Thank you, Doctor. I do have one last question, if you don't mind. Did you see anyone talking to Angela?"

He thought for a moment, and then said, "She had a drink at the bar with Ralph and Mary Hartwell, just a quick one, and Ruth Archer stopped her in the foyer just as she was leaving. They spoke for a moment or two, but that was it."

All three of us rose to our feet. Kate and I gave him

our thanks and said our goodbyes. He was already hurrying away down the corridor when we left.

"So," I said, when we were back in the Maxima. "What do you think?"

Kate shook her head, sighed, and said, "I think the plot's thickening, Harry. I'm wondering if the chief will go for an exhumation of Regis's body."

"Why? He said that only GHB would show in the hair, and I would have thought that even that would be unlikely after all this time."

"True.... But I wonder."

"What?"

"I'll tell you later. We're going to see Ralph now, right?"

I nodded.

"Good. You do the interview. I'll chime in when I think I need to, and I *will* need to. When I do, just play along with me, okay?"

You've got a plan. A sneaky plan, I shouldn't wonder.

I put the Maxima in gear and we headed out.

11

Ralph Hartwell lived on Timberlinks Drive on Signal Mountain, about a thirty-minute drive from the hospital. We were cutting it close. In fact, we arrived five minutes late.

"Good afternoon, Mr. Hartwell. I'm Harry Starke. I called yesterday and we set up an appointment...."

"That you did," he said, obviously in a foul mood. "And I've been doing a little digging. You're quite well known in these parts, but you're not with the police. Why are you here, Mr. Starke? I almost called and canceled the appointment. I don't have to talk to you. I only agreed to do so because I owe it to my brother to help in any way I can with Angela's death. That is why you're here, isn't it?"

Now that's a strange question to ask. Why else would I be here? Methinks maybe you have something else to worry about.

Kate stepped forward, badge in hand. "I'm Lieutenant Catherine Gazzara, Chattanooga PD. Mr. Starke is my associate, a licensed private investigator, and he's consulting with me on the investigation into Angela Hartwell's murder. Thank you for agreeing to talk to us."

Hartwell was taken aback. He waited for her to continue. She didn't. Instead, she took a deep breath and stepped passed him into the foyer.

"We won't take up much of your time, sir. Is there somewhere we can sit and talk?"

At first, he didn't move, and I thought he was going to ask us to leave, but then he seemed to get a grip on himself.

"Yes, of course," he said. "Please follow me."

He led us through the kitchen into his office. It was a big, plush room, lined with bookshelves. A large walnut desk, two Chesterfield easy chairs, and couple more high back guest chairs stood against the far wall

"Please, sit down," he said. "Can I get you a beverage? Coffee, perhaps?"

We declined, and sat on the two guest chairs; he sat behind his desk and leaned back, his elbows resting on the chair's arms, his hands clasped together in front of him, and he was projecting an attitude. I'd known him less than two minutes and already I knew I didn't like him. I also had a feeling it was a mutual dislike.

He wasn't a big man, but it was easy to tell that he was used to having things his way. Even though he was at home, he was wearing a suit—by the cut, a very expensive suit. His fair hair was perfectly coifed, receding at the temples, parted on the right. He was clean-shaven, but the sideburns were just a little too long. His nose was a little too small, his eyes blue and close-set. They stared at me from behind small, gold-rimmed glasses. It was a mean face.

"Mr. Starke would like to ask you some questions, if that's all right," Kate said.

Again, I thought he was going to refuse, but he didn't; he nodded, dropped his chin a little, and stared at me over his hands. I took out my digital recorder, turned it on, and set it on the desk in front of him. I could see he didn't like it, but he didn't object.

"How close were you to Angela Hartwell, sir?" I asked.

"Not close at all, really. She was my brother's wife. I saw her once in a while, to say hello. Usually at the club. Other than that, nothing. That evening was one of those times."

"The company had nothing to do with her. As to family... no."

"You didn't like her, did you?"

"If you must know, no I didn't. She was... how shall I put it? A snooty bitch. Even when Regis was alive, she had little to do with my family."

"She was a total bitch," a voice said.

I looked around. The woman I assumed to be Mary Hartwell walked past my chair and sat down in one of the Chesterfields.

She wasn't at all what I'd expected. She had a light build, and blond hair that was obviously an expensive salon job, hanging dead straight about six inches past her shoulders. Her bangs drew a sharp line just above her eyebrows. Her face was pale and she was scowling. She wore a form-fitting, sleeveless black dress cut a couple of inches above the knee.

Ralph smiled at her, exposing a perfect set of brilliant white teeth.

I waited a moment and then, when neither of them spoke, I continued.

"You called her a bitch. From my conversations with her friends, I didn't get that impression. Why do you say that?"

Ralph opened his mouth to speak, but it was his wife who answered.

"Dear Angela had no time for us. She didn't think we were good enough for her or for her friends, or even the club, and she made it quite plain to one and all whenever she could. She deliberately excluded us from her social gatherings and, when she could get away with it, even from bank functions."

"Why was that, do you think?" I asked.

"She was close to Jennifer, Ralph's first wife. She thought I broke up that marriage. I didn't. It was her that was playing around, not Ralph. Their marriage was over when Ralph and I began seeing each other."

I made a note on my iPad to check that out, but I didn't pursue it.

"I have to ask you this; it's routine," Kate said. Where were you Wednesday evening, the twenty-fifth, between nine thirty and midnight?"

Ralph's eyes narrowed, but he didn't look the least bit uncomfortable.

"Hmmm, the twenty-fifth...." He flipped through a

few pages of his desk calendar. "Last Wednesday. Mary and I were here all evening. I caught up with some work I'd brought home. Then we had a couple drinks and went to bed, around ten thirty, I think. Mary can tell you. She remembers those things better than I do."

We both looked at Mary.

"Yes, ten thirty," she said distantly, looking at her fingernails.

"So when did you last see her?"

"Oh I don't know," Ralph replied, impatiently, "a week, maybe ten days ago, at the club. I didn't note the date and time."

"What if I told you that you both were seen with her at the club on the night she died?"

He looked at Mary, questioningly.

"That's not possible...." He flipped through the desk calendar again. "Oh, wait. Yes. You're right. I was looking at the wrong week. We were at the club that evening. She was just about to leave. I bought her a drink. We had a few words, and she left; maybe twenty minutes in all."

"What time would that have been?"

"Late...ish, for us that is. Nine o'clockish. We're normally out of there by nine."

"And what did you talk about?"

"The usual. Her obsession with Regis' death. We tried to make nice, but she wouldn't have it. Anyway, she left, and so did we, a few minutes later, and went home."

"You don't seem too upset that she's dead."

Neither one of them answered. It was time to step on some toes.

"You inherit everything, don't you? Money, property,

investments, the lot." I asked, keeping a close watch on his eyes.

He smiled at me. "A bit like winning the lottery, you might say."

Damn. That's some kind of attitude.

Okay, that wasn't quite what I was expecting. I looked sideways at Kate. The look on her face was a picture. I decided to dive right in.

"Mr. Hartwell. There's a rumor that Angela thought that you were responsible for your brother's death."

Again, he didn't seem bothered by the question.

"Angela was very disturbed...."

"She was a goddamn nut case is what she was," Mary interrupted angrily. "She spread that vicious lie all over town. If I'd had my way, we'd have sued her for defamation."

"As I said," Ralph continued, unfazed by his wife's outburst. "Angela was very disturbed. I suggested to her that she might need help. I even suggested a good psychiatrist, but she insisted on continuing with her inflammatory accusations. He was my brother. I loved him. Why would I want to kill him?"

"I can think of several reasons," Kate said, "including the fact that he was going to sell the company to one of the big banks. If he did, you would be out in the cold: no job, no credit, and no prospects."

"Rumors," he said. "Just rumors. It would never have happened." He sounded unconcerned, but he was no longer smiling.

"It's also been said," Kate said, "that you killed Angela. Did you?"

"Oh... my... God," Mary looked stunned. "Why would my husband want to kill her?"

"Well she *was* looking into her husband's death. There's that, and I can think of fifty-seven million more reasons," Kate said, staring her in the eye.

"You mean Angela's money?" Ralph said, still smiling. That's the most outrageous thing I've ever heard. Why would I need her money? I already owned the company. It's worth close to a billion. Hah, you're out of your minds. I think it's time you left."

"It's also been said," Kate said, "that before Regis Hartwell suffered his heart attack, you were stealing from the company."

Now that did get a reaction. They both sat up straight in their chairs. She was livid with anger, but Ralph had gone white.

"How dare you?" he asked. His voice, now low, had an edge to it. "How dare you come into my house and make such accusations. Get out. Get out now."

Neither of us moved.

"She told a friend that she had proof you were stealing from the banks," I said. "She also said that Regis had had proof, and that she'd found it, and that he'd confronted you with it. She was convinced you murdered Regis. If it's true there was proof you were stealing from the bank, it's only a matter of time before we find it. I think you might want to consider the consequences of that." *Whew. Did I really say that? We had nothing other than gossip.*

"*Get... out!*" He stood, his face white, his hands shaking, though from fear or from anger I didn't know. "You, lieutenant. I'm going to file a complaint with your superiors. You... you—you...." He was spluttering. He couldn't finish whatever it was he wanted to say. Finally he collapsed back down into his chair. I hear a beeping sound. I looked around. Mary was punching a number into her cell phone.

"Daniel," she said. "I have a police officer and a private detective here in my home making all sorts of wild accusations.... Yes, about Regis.... Yes, Angela too. Can you come. Thank you, Daniel. Yes, I'll make it clear." She disconnected. "That was our lawyer, Daniel Drake," she told me. "He's on his way, Ralph." She stood, walked behind the desk, put her hand on his shoulder, and said. "Daniel says we are not to answer any more questions until he gets here."

I rose to my feet, smiling. "That's fine. I think we have all we need, for now." That last bit I said with a predatory grin. There was no doubt the pair of them were thoroughly unnerved. "Oh, and please give Donald my best."

"Donald?" Mary asked. "Who the hell is Donald?"

"Oh," I said, still smiling, "didn't you know? That's what his friends call him. DD. You know, Daniel Drake... Donald Duck." *They don't call him that, at least not to his face, but what the hell.*

I knew Drake well. He was a sleazy, sharp, and very expensive lawyer with offices near mine. I'd run up against him quite a few times over the past fifteen years. Our relationship, if you could call it that, went back to the days when I was a cop. We were always adversaries. If we were keeping score—I wasn't, but he might have been—I would be up about five to two. He didn't like me, and the feeling was mutual.

"Lieutenant," I said. "We'll leave. DD won't allow these good folks to talk even when it's in their best interests to do so."

She was already on her feet. I grabbed the recorder from his desk, thanked them both, and then turned toward the door. Time for a little Colombo.

"Oh by the way." I almost laughed when I said it, it was so cliché. "It seems that Regis may have died from an injection of potassium chloride. We've already applied for an exhumation order. We'll be in touch to let you know what we find." A lie, but I so enjoyed telling it.

His face was as white as his shirt. Mary looked like she'd been hit by a truck.

Back in the car, I started laughing.

"What" Kate asked. "What's so damned funny?"

"Did you see the looks on their faces when I told them we were going to exhume Regis?

"Yes, damn it. You stole my thunder. I told you when we left Dr. Gray that I'd tell you what I had on my mind later. That was it, you ass. I was about to tell him the same damn thing when you beat me to it."

"Well, Katie," I said affably, "you know what they say: 'Great minds think alike.'"

"Hah! Okay. So what do you think?"

"Well, for a start, I don't think they like each other; not at all. They have no alibi, and they do have the best motive in the world; several of them, in fact: money, power, hate, greed, you name it. And they lawyered up. By the way, DD Drake and I don't get along.

"Yes, I'd say they killed him," I said, "or hired it out. My God, I thought he was going to have a heart attack himself, and her. I think she might have wet herself. If they did kill him, they probably had something to do with Angela's death too, though proving either one is going to be a nightmare. We have nothing."

She nodded. "That's one nasty pair, too. They're made for each other, that's for sure."

I nodded, "They are indeed. How about you, Kate? What's your take on it?"

She sat quietly for a moment, thinking, then said, "I think you're probably right. I think he's good for his brother's death. Exactly how he pulled it off... well, your guess is as good as mine. And if he is, it makes sense that he's responsible for Angela's death too. It's how they died that bothers me most—bizarre, both those deaths. So, where do we go from here?"

"We need more, much more," I said. More footwork. Good old fashioned police work. You up for it?"

She sighed, then said, "I'm slammed, Harry. I'll do what I can...."

"Yeah, I know. Me too. Look, if Angela did have proof that Ralph was stealing from the banks, it has to be somewhere. We have to find it. What about CSI? You were going to see if they found anything at her apartment."

"Yes, I did. Let's go talk to them."

"I've got a better idea," I said. "I'm starving. Let's go get something to eat and then go talk to them."

"That sounds good," she said. "I'm thinking maybe we should also talk to Regis's lawyers. They would have been handling any potential sale, and his will, Angela's too, probably. If he talked to anyone, it would be them, right?'

"Good thought. We need to find out who they are. I'll get Tim on it." I hit the Bluetooth, made the call and gave the instructions. He said he'd call me back as soon as he had something. So, where do you want to eat?"

_____

12

We stopped at Zaxby's on Signal Mountain Road for lunch; I love their chicken tenders. We'd barely gotten seated when my cell phone buzzed. I looked at the screen. It was Tim with the lawyer's name and contact information.

"Creswell and Hughes," I said to Kate when I got off the phone. "I know them. I've done a few jobs for them over the past several years. Gene Creswell handled the Hartwells, and I know him quite well. I'll see if I can get us in to see him."

I made the call, and an appointment for three thirty that afternoon. In the meantime, we'd have just enough time to drop by the PD and check in with CSI.

We could see through the plate glass window of the lab at the Police Services Center on Amnicola that it was a hive of activity. A half dozen techs in white lab coats worked at different stations.

"Hey Lieutenant, Harry," Michael Willis said. "I don't have much for you, I'm afraid."

Willis had been handling most of the CSI operations at the PD even before I joined the force back in 1997. He was a strange little wizard then, and he's grown even more eccentric over the years. He's short, overweight, a little on the scruffy side—clean, but untidy—head shaved and shiny, eyebrows thick and bushy. His hands are... huge. He was one of those people that always seemed to be in a hurry. Even so, he was patient, and always took the time to make sure we understood exactly what he was telling us. He would go through a report word by word until he was sure we had it. And he was a talker.

"The place had been thoroughly turned over," he said. "Clothes, personal items, scattered everywhere. Kitchen drawers turned out onto counter tops, cupboards ransacked, bedding, cushions, even the carpet had been pulled up."

"Any trace?" I asked.

"There was nothing at the crime scene other than what was on the body. We searched almost an acre of golf course, but... nothing. No tire impressions except from other golf carts. Maybe they used one of those to transport her. It would be a job to figure that out, though. They have more than a hundred of them. We did find a single blonde hair caught in the buckle of her watch band, probably a woman's, She was a brunette, right?"

I nodded. "DNA?"

"The follicle was present, so yes, but I have to send it to the lab, so we're looking at several weeks before I can give you a result."

. . .

"What about the apartment?"

"Not much, I'm afraid. There were two glasses on the draining board. They'd been washed and left to drain, so they probably had nothing to do with whoever turned the place over. They might have washed them, but the type of person we're dealing with wouldn't bother to put them out to drain so neatly, would they?"

I shook my head. "Who knows. How about the clothing she was wearing? Anything there? Doc Sheddon said there was some bruising where she wore her watch, that it might have been caused by her being dragged by her wrists. Maybe there are prints on the watch."

"I have her personal belongings. Oh, and we did find her shoes on the golf course: a pair of Tory Burch slip on sneakers. She wasn't wearing much in the way of clothing. Just a shirt, bra and shorts, but as I said, she *was* wearing a David Yurman Albion watch. Expensive, but not excessively so—probably a fashion statement. Anyway, as I said before, we found the hair but nothing else. The crystal was clean—no prints—it must have been wiped, because no watch crystal I've ever seen is that clean. The band was sodden. I guess it had been in the water eight or ten hours, but I'm going to put it through the Pathtech, see if we can find anything."

. . .

"**P**athtech? What's that?" I asked.

Willis grinned. "It's a new toy, a bench-top *fingerprint vacuum metal deposition system.* Well, it's not new. I got lucky. They cost around $30,000, but I found a used one for less than eight and managed to talk the powers that be into letting me buy it. Haven't had it long."

"Oh, how does that work...?" I stopped myself, but it was too late. Oh hell. Big mistake.

"We place the object in the vacuum chamber. The air is sucked out to create a vacuum, and a minute amount of gold is evaporated to form a very thin layer of metal that's distributed over the surface of the item and penetrates any fingerprint deposits, if there are any. The same amount of zinc is then also evaporated in the chamber. The zinc binds to the gold and voila, up comes the print. Well, it's a bit more complicated than that, but you get the idea."

"Gold? Isn't that expensive?" Kate asked.

"Er... yes. So we have to use it sparingly. But, as we have so little to go on in this case, I think it's warranted. If there's anything there, I should be able to let you know tomorrow. I wouldn't hold out too much hope, though. It's a long shot."

We thanked him and left him to it.

We were on our way out to the reception area when we bumped into Chief Johnston.

"Oh hell," Kate whispered. "Here we go."

"Hello, Harry." The look he gave me wasn't too friendly. "What's going on, Lieutenant?"

"Just checking in with Willis, Chief. We're on our way to interview Angela Hartwell's attorney."

"Isn't that what we're *not* paying you to do, Harry?" His attempt at humor—or maybe it was sarcasm—didn't work for me. The strange thing is, we'd always gotten along well when I was on the force. He was an assistant chief then. Maybe he resented me leaving and going out on my own. I know why he lets Kate use me as a consultant; he knows I get results and that it costs him nothing. One day I was going to start billing him.

"That it is," I replied, "and I hope I'm providing value for no money."

He grinned. "Good one, Harry. So, Lieutenant. How goes the investigation?"

"We have a few leads. But it takes time, sir, you know that."

He nodded. "I do, but time is something we're short on. So get it done, close it out, and let's move on. No wild goose chases, you hear, Harry? I appreciate you helping out. You have a nose for this kind of crap, and always have, but I need this one wrapped up, and soon. Later, Lieutenant."

He nodded to us, then walked to the elevator and punched the button.

13

W e arrived at the offices of Creswell and Hughes at exactly three thirty that afternoon. I slipped a half-dozen quarters into the parking meter and we went inside. The receptionist had to call Creswell out from his office, but he wasn't long.

In fact, he came down the corridor almost at the run, his hand outstretched. "Harry Starke." I took it. His grip was firm, and he grasped my left arm with his other hand as I did so. It was a warm and friendly greeting.

"It's great to see you. Always is. And you too, Lieutenant. Come on, come on. We'll go to my office. I think I know what this is all about."

His office was the picture of opulence, of a very successful private practice. But then, he did specialize in corporate law. Which must have been where he'd gotten the money to put himself under the knife, too, because he looked much younger than his sixty years.

"So, Harry. Talk to me," he said briskly, as we all took

seats in front of his desk. "This is about the Hartwells, right?"

Hartwells. Plural. Interesting.

"That's right," I said, "but we're primarily concerned with Angela. We understand that you looked after her legal affairs."

He nodded. "I did, and those of her husband, and his company, the Hartwell Community Banks. What do you need to know?"

"First, if you could give us a brief rundown of...."

"Of course. I handled all of old man Hartwell's affairs after Reggie Hughes died. Up until then, he had handled everything. The corporate structure was already in place when I took over. It was simply a matter of handling the company's everyday needs. Hartwell married late in life, so his children were of an age where worldly experience was, shall we say, not fully developed, and he knew that. He also knew that his youngest son, Ralph, was a bit of a waster, not at all like Regis. Thus, when he put his affairs in order, he made provisions for Ralph but gave control of the company to Regis, and set the whole thing up as a family trust with Regis as the sole executor. When he died, everything passed to Regis, much to Ralph's eternal resentment. No, that's too mild a word. Ralph was very bitter, and he hated his father for what he perceived to be an injustice; he hated Regis for cheating him out of his birthright. I think those were the actual words he used. It only got worse when Regis died and left all of his worldly goods to Angela. Oh, he gained control of the company, but not Regis's money, which was substantial."

"So you're saying that Ralph hated both Regis and Angela?" Kate asked.

"He did indeed."

"And Angela's money and assets all passed to Ralph when she died?"

"Exactly. Ralph is now a very wealthy man."

"Regis died of a heart attack," I said, "but Angela thought he'd been murdered. What do you think?"

"She said as much to me. There may have been something to it. Ralph certainly has a violent streak in him, but... I don't know. What I *can* tell you is that Regis had caught Ralph stealing from the banks, and that Regis was trying to sell the company. I was handling the negotiations."

"You said he had *caught* Ralph stealing," I said. "Was he sure? Did he have proof?"

"Said he did. Though I never saw it."

"Did he say how much?"

He looked at me for a long moment, then said, quietly, "Not exactly. I don't think he had an exact figure. Several million dollars was what he said."

"Whoa," Kate said. "How the hell did that happen?"

"He didn't tell me that either, but I think it had something to do with the corporate customers. He was somehow robbing them, but how...." He trailed off, looked at Kate, then at me.

I thought for a minute, then asked him, "Okay, so if Regis had proof that Ralph was stealing and in such large quantities, why didn't he go to the police?"

"I asked him that myself. The first and most important reason, he said, was that he was trying to protect his company's reputation. Should the thefts be discovered, it would destroy the banks' credibility. I could understand that. Second, he didn't want to destroy his family. Sending Ralph to jail would certainly have done that. Finally, he was protecting the pending sale of the company. A major scandal would have jeopardized it. He told me he was covering the shortfalls himself.

"But the sale didn't go through," Kate said.

"No, it didn't. Regis's death put a stop to it. Ralph didn't want to sell."

"And any chance Ralph might have to pay for his sins died with Regis," I said.

Gene didn't answer. He leaned back in his chair, his elbows resting on its arms, his hands clasped together with two fingers extended to his lips, and he just looked at me, a slight smile on his face.

"What was the asking price for the company?" I asked.

"Regis was sticking at $185 million, just under three times assets."

"So," I said, "if the sale had gone through, Regis would have become extremely wealthy and Ralph would have been exposed as a thief?"

"Wealthy? Yes, he would. But I don't think he would have exposed Ralph. Ralph might have thought so, but Regis wouldn't have let it happen. He told me he was going settle some money on him, enough for the two of them to live comfortably, and then let him go. So tell me, Harry. Was Regis murdered?"

"I don't know," I said. "If I was a betting man, I'd say yes. Unfortunately, there's no way of knowing. If he did, he got away with it. The autopsy report shows the cause of death as a heart attack. Angela, on the other hand, was definitely murdered. She was strangled and dumped in the river."

"And you think Ralph murdered her?" he asked.

"At this point, I don't know that either," I said. "He certainly had the motive—several of them actually, from what I've heard. He doesn't have an alibi, and neither does his wife. We think there probably was tangible proof of his thieving, and that Angela was in possession of it, but we can't find it, and it seems neither can her killer, or killers.

"Gene," I said. "Are you sure Regis never mentioned exactly how Ralph was stealing from the banks?"

"No, he didn't."

"Well, we'll never prove he killed Regis, but if we can find the proof that Ralph was stealing from the bank, whatever it was, if it even existed, maybe we can nail him for that. If he killed Angela.... Well, that's what I'm going to find out. If he did, I'll get him. If he didn't, I'll get whoever did. That I promise you."

"Well," he said, "I wish you the best of luck. If there's anything at all I can do to help, please feel free to call on me. I knew Regis since he was a boy, and Angela for more than ten years. I'd like to see them get the justice they deserve."

We thanked him for his time and help, and then we left. We arrived back at my car just as the meter was about to run out. It was almost five o'clock.

"What do you think?" I asked as I pressed the car's starter.

"I think we have a classic case," she said. "You and I both know that in any murder investigation, the prime suspects are those closest to the victims. In this case, Ralph Hartwell, and maybe his wife, too."

I nodded. "You want to get something to eat?"

"Thanks, but I can't. I still have five hours left of my shift. Would you mind dropping me back at the PD?"

I didn't mind, and I did, and then I drove slowly back to the office. When I'd pulled up in the gated lot, I called my father instead of going in. He was still at his office.

"Hey, Dad. What are you doing for dinner tomorrow?"

"Rose and I are going to the club. Why?"

"I thought I might join you, if that's okay."

"Of course. I'm sure Rose will be delighted to see you."

I didn't think so. Rose, Rosalind, is my stepmother. She's only four years older than me, so you can imagine what that's like. She could be my damned sister.

"That sounds good," I said. "What time?"

"How about seven thirty? Will Amanda be joining us?"

For some reason, my father had taken a real shine to Amanda. They just got along well together—they were alike in many ways. Both driven, both go-getters, both had amazing sense of humors.

"No, she's working. She's doing both broadcasts: six and eleven."

"Well," he said, "maybe next time. I'll see you in the lounge at seven thirty tomorrow evening. *Click.*

Damn, I wish he wouldn't do that. I hadn't finished.

I really had no desire to go into my office. It had been a long day, and it was far from over. I hit the Bluetooth again and called Jacque. Without telling her I was outside, I answered a couple of questions, then told her to lock up and go home. Me? I too headed home. I needed a drink and a shower, and then maybe another drink.

14

The sun was setting in a blaze of red, orange, and gold as I headed out Wednesday evening. It was warm, and the club was bustling—unusual for mid-week.

"Harry, over here." They were in my favorite spot, at the table in the bay window overlooking the ninth green, and they weren't alone. Ruth Archer was seated next to my father and, by the look on her face, Rose wasn't at all happy about it.

"Hello, Dad, Rose, Ruth," I said, dropping onto the curved bench beside Ruth, opposite my stepmother. *Never, I say never, will I ever get used to that idea 'my stepmother.'*

"We were just talking about you," August said. "Ruth was wondering how the investigation was going."

Was she now.

"Which one?" I asked innocently. "I have more than a dozen going."

Ruth reached out and placed her hand on mine. "Oh come on, Harry. You know which one. Angela Hartwell. Everyone in the club is wondering how it's going. We're all agog. Do you have any suspects?"

I withdrew my hand. "I'm sorry, Ruth. I'm not at liberty to discuss an ongoing police investigation. You should know that." I watched her eyes as I said it. They narrowed, almost imperceptibly.

"Oh come on, Harry. You can tell me. Do you have any... *clues?*" She laughed as she emphasized the word, but there was little humor in it.

She really wants to know.

"As I said, I can't discuss it, other than to say it's moving right along. Rose, my love. How are you? I haven't seen you in an age. What have you been up to?" I was watching Ruth as I said it, and again she made with the eyes. Rose began to prattle on about her activities, which were numerous—and boring. I paid lip service to what she was saying, but Ruth was much more interesting. I decided to play her a little.

I waited until there was a break in Rose's narrative and then said, "Ruth, I understand you're in the auto business. How is that going for you?"

"It's going fine, thank you. So are the other businesses in the group...." She paused. "Look, Harry. If you don't mind, could we have a word alone?" She stood, towering above the table. I nodded and got to my feet too.

She picked up her clutch from the table. "Let's go out on the terrace for a moment. You don't mind, do you August? We'll be but a minute, and then I'll return him to you."

August nodded, and I followed her out onto the terrace. It was almost dark, though the night was for the most part clear. There was a half-moon in the sky just to the east, and the stars glittered, obscured now and then by the odd high-flying cloud. If it hadn't been for whom I was with, it would have been quite romantic. I should have been excited. The goddess was dressed to kill. She was wearing a sleeveless, low-cut, flimsy summer dress and heels that put her eyes almost two inches above my own. I have to admit, as big as I am, I was a little intimidated.

"So, Harry," she said, linking her arm with mine and steering me to the steps that led down to the eighteenth green. "I hope you don't mind. I wanted to talk to you about Angela. You do know she was a good friend of mine, don't you?"

I didn't, and I said so.

"Well she was. A very good friend. We were so close in so many ways."

Jeez, that's the first I've heard of it.

"Go on," I said, more than a little curious.

"Well, she'd not been herself since Regis died. I know she had a lot on her mind, and I was worried about her. There's a rumor going around that she thought Regis had been murdered. I couldn't believe it. Could it have been true, do you think?"

"When did she tell you this?"

"Well, when I heard the rumor, of course I asked her about it. She confirmed it. Did you know about it?"

I smiled to myself. "I did. What else did she tell you?"

"Oh, nothing. She just said she was certain someone

had killed him and that she was determined to find out who."

"You said you knew Angela well?" I asked, skeptically. She didn't seem to notice.

"Yes. I just told you. I knew her very well. We were good friends. I knew Regis very well, too, and, of course I know Ralph too.... So, Harry, you know about her... quest, I suppose it was? What do you think? Was Regis murdered?"

"Maybe. At this point in the investigation, I don't know, but I intend to find out, and when I do, I'll put the killer away for the rest of his—or her—days," I said, pointedly. "But, tell me, Ruth. Why are you so interested?"

"Oh, I'm just curious. You said 'her'.... Do you think it could have been a woman?"

"Why not?" I paused. "Ruth, you were at the club the night she was killed.... Oh, no," I said, smiling, as her eyes widened, "you're getting the wrong idea. I was just going to ask if you saw her with anybody."

"Oh. I see. She was with Doctor Gray for more almost an hour before she left, and she had a quick drink with Ralph and Mary. They were talking. About what, I have no clue."

"How do you know they were talking? Were you watching them?"

"*H*arry, no." She sounded outraged. "I know because I was seated at the bar just behind them. My lord, you have a suspicious mind."

"You spoke to her in the lobby, when she was leaving. What was that about?"

"Wow, you have been digging around. I asked her how she was doing. She said fine, and that was about it. She left, and I left too." She stopped talking for a moment, and we continued walking on past the eighteenth green in silence, into the growing darkness.

Eventually she spoke again. "She was my friend, Harry, and if there's anything I can do to help... well, you only have to ask." And then she took me completely by surprise. As she said it, she turned and stepped in front of me, put both arms around my neck, and kissed me—a deep, lingering kiss that took my breath away. I was so damned surprised that I just let it happen. Then I came to my senses. I grabbed her by both arms and pushed her away, none too gently.

She laughed, a deep gurgling sound I could almost feel.

"You have no idea how much I've been wanting to do that, Harry Starke."

And I had to admit, it was kinda good. No, it was very good, but I had to nip this thing in the bud. "It was inappropriate, Ruth." I said, "do you have a tissue by any chance?

She laughed again, opened her clutch, took one out, and handed it to me. I wiped my mouth, folded it, and stuck it into my pants pocket.

"Inappropriate am I?

Oh Harry. I've been called some things in my life, but impropriate was never one of them. Don't you like me?"

"It's not a case of liking you. Of course I do."

"But not enough to...?"

"No. Not enough for that."

"Is it because of that little skank Amanda Cole?"

Whoa! What the hell brought that on? "Yes, it's Amanda," I snapped, "and she's not a skank. Far from it. And *that* was inappropriate too. Now, if you don't mind, we'll go back inside."

She nodded, but said nothing, just turned and began to walk. I remained where I was. She stopped and turned to look at me.

"Well, are you coming or not? Or are you going to stand there and sulk for the rest of the night?"

When we got back inside, she placed her hand on my arm, and said, "Please remember. If there's anything I can do to help. I will. Now, I have to rejoin my sisters. It's the end of the month, and we always get together for dinner. Would you like to meet them?"

Well, what could I say to that? To refuse would have been inappropriate—there was that damned word again—and besides, I was curious.

They were already seated at their table. I'd heard they were twins, but I wasn't expecting this. Nope, they weren't dressed alike, but that was the only difference. They were both blondes. Both had their hair in ponytails. Their makeup was exactly the same, even down to the eyeliner and... yes, they were beautiful.

"Rachel, Rebekah; this is Harry Starke. Harry, these are my sisters."

"Um, it's nice to meet you both," I said. They stood and shook my hand, first one and then the other. They were not as tall as their sister, by a good four inches. I have to tell you, their sameness was uncanny, unnerving. I looked at Ruth; she had an enigmatic, tongue-in-cheek smile on her face.

"Okay," I said to Ruth. "I know you've heard it a thousand times, but how do you tell them apart?"

"I don't really know," she said. "I can, of course, but sometimes I do get it wrong. When I do, I think it's because they want me to. Isn't that right?"

They both laughed. Even that sounded the same.

"Please, Mr. Starke," Rebekah said. At least, I think it was Rebekah. Ruth had introduced them in that order. "Come and sit down. Talk to us. We've heard so much about you. You're quite famous, and oh-so handsome."

"Yes, he is," Rachel said. "No wonder Ruth is so taken with you."

"Bekah, Rachel, please. You're embarrassing me."

The hell they were. Why do I suddenly get the feeling I'm being set up? "I'd love to sit and talk," I said. *You'd better believe it.* "Unfortunately, my father and his wife are waiting for me. I really do need to get back to them. Some other time, perhaps?"

"Of course," Ruth said. "Thank you for taking the time to talk to me, and for... well, you know," she said, looking down at me.

Sheesh. That's a first.

"And, please don't forget, if I can help...."

When I rejoined my father and Rose, I glanced at them from across the dining room. They were all seated, heads together, talking quietly.

"What was that all about?" August asked.

"I think Wonder Woman was on a fishing trip."

"I'm sure she was," Rose said dryly. "You have lipstick on your mouth." *I do? I thought I'd got it all.*

"Damn," I said. "Please excuse me while I go and clean up." Yep, she was right. I did. I cleaned it off in the bathroom, made sure there was none on my shirt, then made my way back between the tables.

"So what did she want?" Rose asked.

"She wanted to know how the investigation was going.... It was... weird."

"How so?" August asked.

"She kept saying how close she and Angela were, but that was the first I'd heard of it. Have you any such?"

He shook his head. I looked at Rose. She smiled and mouthed, "No."

"So why would she tell me she was? And what the hell is she after?" I was talking to myself, and they were rhetorical questions that required no answers, but....

"Maybe she's involved somehow," Rose said. It was something that had been wandering unbidden through my own subconscious mind, a thought I'd pushed away, but....

I sat for a moment, thinking. Then I pushed my chair back and stood up. "I need for you to excuse me for a minute," I said. They both looked up at me and nodded. "I'm going to see if I can get another invite to the Archer's table. I turned them down a few minutes ago. Do me a favor, Dad. Keep an eye on me and back my play."

I walked across the room, ostensibly heading for the bar, but wending my way between the tables, stopping now and then to say hello to friends until finally I reached the Archer table.

"Ladies," I said affably, trying to act as if I were a little under the influence. "I was just on my way to the bar. Can I buy you all a drink?"

"Only if you sit with us while you drink it," Rebekah said. Or was it Rachel?

"Er... well, I was...." I made a show of turning to look back at our table. August was watching; so was Rose. I pointed to my chest and then at the empty chair at the Archer's table. He waved a hand, smiled, and nodded.

"Okay," I said. "How lucky can one get? Three lovely creatures all in one spot. But only for a minute. Can't neglect my stepmother." I winked at them as I said it. "What would you like to drink?" They told me. I went to the bar and asked Joe to deliver them.

"So," I said, sitting down beside Ruth, facing the twins. "What do you want to talk about?"

"Why Angela, of course." I don't know which one said it. Rachel, I think. "This place is literally buzzing with it. When are you going to arrest the killer?" She was laughing as she said it, but there was something about the look on her face that sent a chill down my spine. This girl, was not like Ruth. Maybe neither of them were. They had an edge to them, something I couldn't put my finger on.

"I don't know who the killer is... *yet*." I said, emphasizing the word.

"Oh come on, Mr. Starke. You must have some idea. Do tell."

"No, really. It's still too early in the investigation," I said, looking up at Joe as he delivered the drinks.

"Ruth tells me that she and Angela were great friends. Did you girls know her too?"

"Of course we did." This time it was the other girl—Rebekah?—who answered. "We were all friends. In fact, I do a lot of business with Ralph Hartwell. I run Archer Finance, among other things. Before Ralph, I used to deal with Regis. Yes, Angela was our friend. Do you think it might have been someone here, at the club?"

So if you run the finance company, you're Rachel. Hmmm. If Ruth can tell you two apart, why did she introduce you as Rebekah? Is she pulling my chain, or what?

"Again," I said, "I don't know. You do a lot of business with Ralph, though?"

She looked up at me through her eyelashes, just like her sister had. "Some. I maintain several accounts at Hartwell, we both do, for all four of our companies." She said it slowly, and somewhat warily.

"Do you know him well?" I asked.

"Yes, I suppose so. Not socially, of course. Through our business dealings, mostly."

"When did you last see Angela... Rachel?" She smiled at my obvious mistake. Yeah, I know. I could play their little game too. It's Rebekah, or is it? We'll see? Why would Ruth want to confuse me? She must have a reason, right?

"Hmmm, last... Tuesday, I think it was. We were here

for lunch. Angela was just leaving when we arrived.... How did you know I was Rachel?"

Now it was my turn to smile. I wasn't sure who the hell she was.

"Maybe you're not as alike as you think you are. Did she speak to you?"

"She said hello." Rachel, if that's who she was, was no longer smiling. "If you'll excuse me," she said, pushing her chair back, "I need to use the facilities. Ruth, will you come with me?" And they left, leaving me alone with... hell, I didn't know. Rebekah? Rachel? *Damn!*

"You must excuse my sister, Mr. Starke. She likes to play games with people. Sometimes I think she has a mean streak. Me, on the other hand, I also like to play with people... if you know what I mean."

And boy did I. The look she was giving me was unmistakable. Her head was dipped slightly, her eyes were narrowed, and the smile offered an invitation that was hard to resist. I ignored it.

"It's Rebekah, right?"

She leaned against the backrest of her chair and folded her hands in her lap, an enigmatic smile on her face, but she said nothing. *It would seem that her sister wasn't the only one who liked to play games.*

"Look, I need to get back to my table. I've neglected them for too long. Please wish your sisters a good evening from me and tell them it's been a pleasure." I got to my feet, pushed the chair under the table, and walked back to my own table. I felt like I'd been put through a wood chipper. I'd already known Ruth was a shark. Now I knew her sisters were barracudas, too.

I didn't linger at the club. It was already after ten, and I wanted to get out of there. I said my goodbyes and left. As I walked toward the foyer, I turned to wave to my father; out of the corner of my eye, I saw the Archers. All three of them were watching me.

15

I arrived home and turned on the TV in the living room just in time to see Amanda close out her segment; it was just after eleven. I hit the speed dial on my cell phone and called her.

"Hey, Harry. You must have been watching me."

"I was. You going home or coming here?"

"Depends on you. Do you have anything to eat?"

"I could knock you something up."

For some reason, that made her laugh. "We'll think of something," she said. "I'll be there in about forty-five minutes. Why don't you open a nice bottle of red?"

"That I can do. See you soon." After I disconnected I wandered into the kitchen and grabbed a bottle of Merlot, opened it, and set it on the counter to breathe. Then I poured myself three generous fingers of Laphroaig Quarter-Cask scotch and walked out onto the patio overlooking the river.

All was quiet. The river was a flat sheet of onyx, the blackness broken only by the reflections of the lights on the Thrasher Bridge in the distance. The vast bulk of Lookout Mountain was silhouetted against the deep violet of the moonlit sky. Somewhere off in the distance, I heard music playing. Mozart's Symphony number 41. It suited my mood perfectly, and that of the river. I settled down on a lounger and was soon lost in thought.

I must have nodded off, because the next thing I knew Amanda was shaking my shoulder.

"Hey you," she said.

I came to with a start, looked around, disoriented.

"Wow," I said. "I was gone for a minute." I shook my head. "How are you? How was your day?"

"Better now that I'm here. More to the point: how was yours?"

I looked down. I still had my drink in my hand. I set it on the table beside the lounger, got to my feet, put my hands on her shoulders, and kissed her, lightly.

"That, my dear, was what I was trying to get a handle on when I came out here. It was productive, at least early on. Then, at the club, it kinda got away from me. I met the rest of Archer family."

"Oh... and...?"

"That's just it. I don't know. They asked a whole lot of questions, more than you'd consider normal, and... Ruth made a pass at me."

"Oh she did? And exactly how did that work?"

"She asked to talk to me in private. We went outside and... she kissed me." You think telling her was a mistake? Yeah, well. Better she got it from me than from someone else.

"She kissed you?" Her voice had nails in it.

"She did, but I pushed her away and told her it wasn't on. What really bothered me, though, was I couldn't figure out what it was all about. You had to be there to understand what I mean?"

"Oh I wish I'd been there all right."

"No, no. That's not what I meant." *Keep working it, Harry. You'll get there in the end.*

"Look, Amanda. There was nothing to it. She took me by surprise is all. Hell Dad and Rose were both there. She was after information. I have the strongest feeling that the Archer family is in some way involved in this mess. I'm sure of it. I was trying to figure it out, before you came home, but I fell asleep."

She looked at me, her face softened, "It's okay. I don't blame you, well, not entirely. I blame her. So what was she after?"

"In a minute. You hungry? No? Wine, then?"

She nodded. I went into the house, poured her a glass, and brought it out to her. She was standing on the edge of the patio, looking out over the river toward the mountain, seemingly deep in thought.

"Penny for them," I said, handing her the drink.

"I've never liked that family. I knew them in high school, and their father was a sleazy little man even then. He was as crooked as he was high. I always thought the girls were a chip off the old block...." She stopped talking, stared out into space, her glass to her lips, her left hand a fist on her right hip.

"Go on," I said.

"They've been involved in some sharp financial practices. At least that's what Charlie Groves says. He has no proof, of course, but I wouldn't bet against him."

"What kind of sharp practices?"

"Car loans, boat loans, mortgages. That finance company they run is little more than a pool full of loan sharks. They skirt the laws. Make loans to people that can't afford to make the payments. They take a large down payment, set interest rates high. If the customer pays, fine. If not, they repossess or foreclose and the borrower loses everything. They employ a couple of heavies to repo the cars and boats and get the courts to foreclose on the real estate, then they start the process over, and resell. No laws are ever broken, at least that we know of. It's a win-win situation. Profitable either way. Charlie reckons they repo more cars and boats than they sell. Weird, huh? So, tell me what happened at the club."

I gave her the full story. I told her my thoughts, especially those about the Archer's fishing for information, first Ruth and then the twins. We talked on into the night, and the more we did, and the more I listened to Amanda's input, the more convinced I became the Archers were somehow connected, but for the life of me I couldn't see how.

"And then there's the fact that, as far as we know," I said, "Ruth was the last person to see Angela alive."

"So what now?" she asked. "Have you talked to Kate?"

"Not yet. I will tomorrow. You asked what next,

though—I've been thinking about that. The first thing to do is to delve deep into the Archer family affairs. I'll get Ronnie on that in the morning. I'd also like to talk to the Crofts and the Bentleys. They were close friends of the Hartwells, or so I've been told. Maybe Angela told them something we don't know." *But, hell. We don't know nothin'!*

"I also need to see if Mike Willis found anything with that Pathtech thing he's so proud of. Hell, I might even give Ruth another chance to grill me. Maybe she'll let something slip. I think maybe lunch at the club is in order."

"Oh I doubt that. She's a smart bi—she's smart. Too damn smart by far to let anything slip." She paused. "When were you planning to do it?"

"I have stuff I need to get done tomorrow, so I thought maybe Friday."

"Tell you what. I don't have to go in to work until three thirty. Why don't I come with you?"

I grinned at her. "There's nothing for you to worry about. I can handle the... bi—all by myself."

"Oh I'm not worried about you. Her? Yes. I'm coming with you. Don't argue."

I smiled and shook my head. Big as Ruth was, I had no doubt that Amanda was a match for her; maybe not physically, but in a battle of words, Ruth wouldn't stand a chance. I said okay and let it go.

Finally, we lay there, quietly, side by side, holding hands and sipping our drinks. Life was good.

16

The following morning, I drove by the PD on my way to the office and handed Willis the tissue I'd used to wipe my mouth after Ruth Archer kissed me. It was a forlorn hope that there might be usable DNA on it, but hell; you never know. I told him it was urgent, and asked him if he could get it expedited. He said he'd give it his best try. I left him staring down at the plastic baggie. I had a good idea of what he was thinking.

So, by the time I arrived at my office the place was already bustling. I didn't linger in the bull pen. I went straight to my inner sanctum and closed the door. I needed a little time alone to think and organize my day.

I didn't get it.

I'd just retrieved a legal pad from the desk drawer when there was knock at the door and Jacque walked in with a cup of coffee in her hand. She placed it in front of me and said, "Daniel Drake called, Mr. Starke. He wants you to call him back."

I grabbed the cup. "I bet he does. Well, he can wait."

"And how long do you expect him to wait? I'll let him know you'll call him... when?" Jacque is a great one for customer service. The problem was, Daniel Drake was not a client, nor would he ever be. Still, whatever Jacque wants, Jacque usually gets.

I heaved a long sigh. There was no getting out of it. "Okay, you win. I'll call him now." I reached for the phone. "Please tell Ronnie I need him." I said, and then dialed the number. "And thanks for the coffee."

Jacque nodded and left the room, closing the door behind her.

"Daniel," I said when he picked up. "I hear you want a word with me. What can I do for you?"

"You can stay away from the Hartwells is what you can do. They are both very upset at the way you and that police officer treated them on Tuesday. You are not, I say *not*, to talk to either one of them again unless I'm present. Do you understand me, Mr. Starke?"

"We're being a bit formal, aren't we Dan? You've always called me Harry in the past."

"This is a formal call, and you should treat it as such. I will brook no further harassment of my client. I say again: do you understand?"

At that point, there was another knock at my door. Ronnie poked his head in. I waved for him to come in and take a seat.

"You wouldn't be recording this conversation without telling me, now would you, Dan?" I said into the phone.

He was silent for a moment.

You sneaky son of a bitch, I thought.

"Well, since you are, I'll make it worth your while. I am investigating, in conjunction with the Chattanooga PD, the homicide of Angela Hartwell. Now, as Ralph Hartwell was, for all intents and purposes, Mrs. Hartwell's next of kin, and did in fact upon her death inherit more than $57 million, he and his wife are at the very least persons of interest and as such are part of the investigation. I will be interviewing them again, several times, I shouldn't wonder, and at my convenience. You are welcome to attend any and all such interviews, should you so desire. Obviously I won't be able to give you advance notice of such interviews, so you should hold yourself ready to receive calls from the Hartwells whenever they feel they might need you."

"You son-of-a—"

"Goodbye, Dan." I disconnected before he could complete his thought.

"So, Ronnie," I said, laying the handset back in its cradle. "How are you this fine morning?"

He looked at me, his eyes wide, obviously taken aback at my good humor.

"Er... fine, Mr. Starke. Jacque said you needed to see me."

"I do. I do indeed. Now, I know you've been looking into the Hartwells' finances. Do you have anything to add to what I already know?"

He shook his head. "No sir, other than the fact that there have been rumors that Ralph may have been involved in some underhand dealings, but those seem to have died down since his brother passed. I haven't been able to find any meat on the bones yet, but I'll keep digging."

"Good. I have another project for you. What do you know about the Archer family and their companies?"

"Not much, sorry. I know who and what they are, and I know they sail very close hauled. I'd say they're loan sharks, and even the word 'usury' might not be too strong, but their business practices are... very profitable. So I understand." He said, sitting up straight in his chair. "Hey, is this about what we were talking about yesterday morning?"

Oh he's quick, is Ronnie. "No, of course not." I said. "I've had a couple of run-ins with the sisters is all, and I was wondering.... No, I wasn't wondering. I need to know everything about them. Can you get on it right away?"

"Yes, sir. How deep do you want me to dig?"

"I want everything. I want to know about their finances, their companies, their social lives, Facebook, Twitter. I want to know what brand of toilet paper they use."

He grinned, gathered up his phone and iPad, and said, getting to his feet, "I'll get right on it."

I waited until he'd closed the door and then punched my iPhone's speed dial for Kate.

"Hey you," she said. "I was just about to call you. What's going on?"

I spent the next ten minutes bringing her up to speed on the last couple days, minus the pass Ruth had made at me. That I didn't need her to know about.

"Kate," I said finally, "I have a deep-seated feeling that the Archers are up to their necks in this thing."

"That famous 'second sight' of yours at work again?"

"Call it what you will. A hunch, maybe. But I can't get them out of my head. Look, I've been a member of the country club for longer than I can remember. I've seen the Archers around once in a while. I didn't know who they were, and I didn't care. Now, over the space of three days I've seen more of them than I have in a year, and they, all three, are showing an unhealthy interest in me and in the investigation.

"And here's another thing. We also know that the Archers do their banking at Hartwell. We know, at least we think we know, that Ralph was robbing the Hartwell Bank's customers, right? So what if the Archers were part of that?"

"That, Harry, would be a hell of a stretch."

"Yeah, well." I sat back in my chair, not a little put out. "Listen, I also called to see if Willis found anything with that fancy new machine of his. I was wondering too if the divers had found the phone, and then I got to think-ing. Those things, iPhones, they back themselves up to the Cloud, automatically, right? Maybe you can pull the backup."

"There's nothing from Willis yet, but he said maybe early this afternoon, I'll have to let you know. No, the divers did not find the phone. As to the iPhone backup, yes, I can get it, but it's not going to be easy. Apple is very protective of customer information. I'm not sure how it works with a deceased's phone, but I'll need a search warrant for sure, which I can get easily enough in this particular case, but the process won't be quick—probably a couple of weeks, and then only if we're lucky."

"How about Angela's apartment? Did CSI find anything new?"

"**The** two glasses were clean, and I do mean **clean. They'd been washed and wiped; they were sparkling. There's no evidence that the apartment was broken into, so either they had a key or she let them in. There were prints everywhere, but none that couldn't be accounted for, except for a few smudges, that is.**"

"Well damn. That's not what I was hoping for. Oh well. That's okay, but we need that Apple backup ASAP. You need to go ahead and get that started. We need to see her emails, texts, call logs, photos, videos, the works."

"Y es, sir. I'll get on it as soon as you hang up, sir."

"Okay, okay. There's no need for the sarcasm. I didn't mean to come off like I was giving orders."

"Hell, Harry. I know that. I was just yanking your chain. Lighten up. Is there anything else, or can I get back to work?"

"Yes, I need to interview a couple club members. Tomorrow, ideally. Do you want to join me?"

"Nope. That's one of the reasons I involved you in this, remember? They're your people. They relate to you, and your status in their world. Better if I stay out of it. Just keep me up to speed, okay? Why don't you take Amanda with you? She gets along with that crowd."

"I might just do that. If you'll get that iPhone thing started...."

"Right away. Bye, Harry." She disconnected.

I made calls to both the Crofts and the Bentleys, but reached neither of them. There was a house sitter at the Crofts who informed me that they were out of the country, had been for more than a month, and they weren't expected back for another three weeks. I left a voicemail for the Bentleys telling them I would be at the club for lunch tomorrow afternoon, Friday, and that I'd like to meet with them.

The rest of the day I spent trying to make some sense of what I knew, which wasn't much.

The only real suspect I had was Ralph Hartwell, and even that was tenuous. He had motive, but hell, Regis was his brother. Yeah, I know. It wouldn't be the first time brother had killed brother. That story was as old as time itself. Cain killed Abel, right? And for far less than to save his sorry ass and a company worth a couple of hundred million. I knew we'd never be able to prove that, but what about his sister-in-law? An extra fifty-seven mill would come in handy.

And then there was Ruth Archer. Maybe her sisters, too. As far as I could tell, Ruth was the last person to see Angela alive, and all three of them had seemed to have an unhealthy interest in what I was doing.

I doodled on the pad, wrote notes, scratched them out, wrote the same notes again, drank coffee until finally I had to quit. My head was aching and I was tired. When I looked at my watch, I saw that it was after five. Time to call it a day and go home.

17

I t was Friday; a beautiful June day, and Amanda and I were seated at my favorite spot, the table next to the big bay window overlooking the ninth green. Amanda was quiet. She seemed to have something on her mind, but wouldn't say what it was. I was watching a foursome make their approach shots to the green.

I say watching. My eyes were on them, but my mind was elsewhere.

"Mr. Starke?"

She was dressed for tennis, perhaps thirty years old, nice-looking, good figure, and her face had a worried look on it.

I blinked at her. "Yes. I'm Harry Starke. What can I do for you?"

"I'm Grace Bentley. I got your voice mail. I'm sorry I didn't get back to you, but I've just returned from Barbados. I didn't know about Angela.... I didn't hear until this morning. I tried to call her cell last night, but it went straight to voicemail. I had a feeling something was wrong, but it wasn't until I arrived here at the club that..." she paused, wiped her eyes, then continued: "that I heard she was dead. Mr. Starke, they tell me you're working with the police on the investigation. Is that true?"

"It is. Please. Sit down. This is Amanda Cole."

"Nice to meet you, Amanda," she extended a hand and Amanda shook it, smiling. "I enjoy watching you on Channel Seven."

"It's nice to meet you too. Would you like a drink?"

Grace shook her head and sat down opposite me, on the far side of the table.

I said, "I've been asked by Lieutenant Catherine Gazzara of the Major Crimes Unit to consult on the case." I reached for my wallet and handed her my card and Kate's. "You can call her. She'll confirm. If you'd rather talk to her, I can call and ask her to see you."

"No, that won't be necessary. I know who you are, and I know your father, August, quite well."

She opened the clutch she was carrying, retrieving something that she then placed on the table in front of me. I picked it up, looked at it, then looked at her.

"Angela gave me that. She was worried for her safety. She asked me, if anything happened to her, to give that to the police. It's the key to a safe deposit box."

I nodded. I could see that it was, and I could also see the number stamped on it: 1003.

"Do you know the bank?" I asked.

"Yes. It's 1st Appalachian, the downtown branch on Broad."

"When did she give you this?"

"Two weeks ago. Just before I left on vacation. I told her not to be silly, but...." She wiped her eyes again.

"You said 'I.' You went by yourself?"

"No, of course not. It was a girls thing; friends from college. We go somewhere every year.

"You obviously knew her very well."

She nodded, still wiping her eyes. "I've known her since we were children. We were in grade school together."

"Did she talk to you about...?"

"About Regis? Of course. She told me everything. She was convinced he was murdered. I was her best friend."

Hmmm. That's two best friends.

"Who did she think murdered him? Did she say?"

"No. All she would say was that there were people involved in Regis's death who would like to see her silenced."

"And she didn't give you any idea who those people might be?"

"No. I asked her several times, but she just said it would all come out soon."

"Did you spend a lot of time with Angela, Mrs. Bentley?"

"Oh yes. Mostly here at the club, but sometimes we'd meet for lunch downtown. She loved the English Rose Café...." She paused to wipe her eyes again, then continued. "We'd meet here two or three times a week, sometimes to play tennis and then have lunch, sometimes for dinner. My husband Jack was a golfing buddy of Regis'. We were very good friends. She confided in me. The last time we were together was here in the club, just before we left on vacation.... She... she said she thought she was being stalked."

Whoa, that's a new twist.

"Why did she think that?" I asked. "Did she say who she thought it might be?"

"No. I asked her, but she said she didn't know, that it was just a feeling that someone was watching her. She also told me that she thought her apartment had been searched, but she wasn't even sure about that. I told her to go to the police, but she said they'd just laugh at her, that they already thought she was a kook."

Hmmm. So she'd already been. Kate never mentioned that. I wonder if she made a complaint. If she did, there'd be a report.

I didn't get it. If she thought she was being stalked, and she was making waves for someone, she must have known she was in danger. Why the hell wouldn't she have reported it?

"Okay," I said. "Now I want you to think very carefully about this next question. Was there anyone here in the club, among the members, that she didn't like, didn't get along with?"

She thought for a moment, then said, "Well, there was Ralph Hartwell, of course. She never got along with him, ever, and toward the end they were barely speaking to one another." She hesitated, then said. "She wasn't keen on the Archer sisters either. I caught her staring at them many times, and you should have seen the looks she gave them."

"Why didn't she like them, do you think?"

"I don't know for sure, but...." She sighed. "Yes I do. She told me she caught Ruth making a pass at Regis. It would have been a week or so before he died. They are not well-liked here, Mr. Starke. From what I've heard, those girls are involved in a lot of shady dealings. They are very wealthy, but... well, there's talk that they didn't come by their money honestly."

"What sort of talk?"

"Mostly from my husband, Jack." She shook her head, obviously reluctant to continue.

"Go on, Mrs. Bentley. It's important."

She sighed again, but went on. "Jack is an auto dealer. He owns the Jack Bentley GM dealership." I nodded. I knew Jack well; played golf with him occasionally. His family had been running a successful business in Chattanooga since the forties.

"Well," she continued. "He knew Ben Archer quite well. In fact, Ben worked for Jack's father, until he fired him. Something to do with spare parts, I think. Anyway, I don't know the ins and outs of it, but Jack's convinced that their entire enterprise is a scam. You'll need to talk to him if you want the details, and even then all you'll get is a lot of conjecture. No one knows much about them, not even Jack." She looked toward the door, then back at me. "Look, Mr. Starke. I need to go. Here's Jack's number. Why don't you give him a call? I'm sure he'll talk to you."

I took the card from her, thanked her, and watched her go. There was something about the stoop of her shoulders, and the way she was wiping her eyes as she walked, that filled me with sadness.

"So, what do you think of all that?" I asked.

"I think you've found yourself a whole nest of worms," Amanda said dryly. "I also think Ruth Archer is more than a bit player. Watch yourself, Harry. That one's a man eater." I grinned at her, but she didn't smile back.

18

Amanda dropped me off at the office at a little after two o'clock and then left to do some shopping. I punched up a cup of Dark Italian Roast coffee and retired to my cave. I had intended to take a few quiet moments to drink it, but I couldn't. I was too restless. I paced back and forth in front of my desk, cup in hand.

I was well used to working alone, had been ever since I left the PD, but, as they say, "no man is an island." I needed someone to bounce things off of. I called Kate, but her phone went straight to voicemail.

Damn!

I went around the desk and dropped heavily into my throne, sat back, put my feet up on the desk, and closed my eyes. Almost instantly, my head was full of images: Angela on her back in the river; Ruth Archer—that was of hell of a kiss she'd laid on me—the twins.

If Regis Hartwell was murdered, and Angela had proof.... If Ralph was robbing the banks, and if Angela had proof.... If he was somehow involved with the Archers, and Angela had proof.... Hell, she had been a dead woman walking any way you cut it.

I turned the safe deposit box key over in my hand. I needed to get ahold of Kate. We needed a search warrant to open the box. I dialed her number again. Voicemail. I left a message asking her to call me, then went back to my thoughts.

Suppose they were... the Archers, working with Ralph. How the hell were they doing it? It had to be something like Ronnie described.... Ralph doesn't seem to be much of a techie, so Internet fraud was probably not the answer. He can't just be taking it right out of customer's accounts. He'd be caught at that in a New York minute, probably quicker. Has to be checks. Has to be....

My thoughts were interrupted as my iPhone began to vibrate its way across the top of my desk. I grabbed it just as it was about to fall off. It was Kate.

"Hey," I said. "Where've you been? I've been trying to reach you."

"I've been in a meeting with the chief. He's not happy. It's been more than a week and we still have nothing concrete for him."

"Jeez, Kate. Tell him he needs to have patience. This is not an easy one. We have no physical evidence, nothing yet from Willis, and no suspects—at least, none we can be sure of. We start harassing Ralph Hartwell or the Archer sisters without cause, and Dan Drake will be all over us. Well, all over me."

"I know, and that's what I told him. Didn't do a whole hell of a lot of good, but.... Well you know Johnston, probably better than I do." She paused, and then her voice brightened. "Hey. I do have one bit of good news. Willis found a partial print on the watchband. If we can find a match, we'll have something solid. He's running it through AFIS as we speak. I'll know something later this afternoon. There's still nothing from the DNA lab about the hair though, and I don't expect there will be for a couple more weeks."

"Well, the print is something," I said. "But if it belongs to who I think it might, there won't be a match in AFIS."

"You're talking Ralph, correct?"

"Yeah. Either him or one of the Archers. Listen, I have something too. I have a key to a safe deposit box that belonged to Angela Hartwell. Can you get a warrant? We need to get into it."

"Where the hell did you get that?"

"I'll tell you when I see you. Look, if you can't get a warrant, I'll call Henry Strange. He'll issue one."

"I can get one. Which bank and branch? I'll also need the box number."

I gave her the information and told her I'd already checked and that the bank was open on Saturday morning. She said she'd give it her best shot. I tried to tell her that calling Judge Strange was the quickest and easiest way anyway, but....

"Let me try it through the proper channels first, Harry. I don't want there to be even a hint of impropriety."

"Since when were you bothered about improprieties?" I asked.

"Since Johnston jumped all over me less than thirty minutes ago. We'll do it my way, okay?"

"Alright, alright."

After we disconnected, I got myself another cup of Dark Italian, asked Jacque to hold my calls, and settled back down in my chair. I stayed there for the next hour.

I think they call it a power nap.

It was after four when I came around. I looked at my watch, and then called Amanda.

"Hey," I said. "You at work?"

"No, I have the day off. Why?"

"You want to get some dinner?"

"We could. Where? When?"

"Somewhere quiet, where you won't be the center of attention."

"I know just the place. Where are you?"

"The office."

"Great. I'll pick you up in forty-five minutes."

Click.

Damn! I'll never get used to that. Whatever happened to "Goodbye?"

She picked me up right on time. I slid into the passenger seat of her Lexus and was immediately taken by how stunning she looked. She was wearing a floaty white summer dress with a flared skirt cut above her knees. It had ridden up and showed almost all of the loveliest pair of thighs this side of the Mississippi. And she was in a great mood. Happy, laughing, joking—and it was infectious. She soon had my own spirits right up there with her own.

"So where are we going?" I asked, as she pulled out of the lot.

"I thought the Mountain City Club would be nice," she said, looking sideways at me as she headed south on Georgia.

"Sure. Why not? I'd been thinking more along the lines of my place, but Mountain City is good."

"Your place? I need real food, and the last time you said you'd cook we ended up with a fast food delivery."

"Fast food my butt. That salmon came straight from Catch of the Day. It was delicious."

"No it wasn't. It was.... You took the easy way out. Now shut up. We're almost there."

She made up for what she said was "fast food" by inhaling a ten-ounce slab of chargrilled North Atlantic salmon and fresh vegetables followed by Key Lime pie and an ice cream sundae. Boy does that girl like her groceries. Me? I had a New York strip steak and a spoonful of Amanda's sundae.

"So," she said, between mouthfuls, "I've been talking to Charlie Grove. I think I may have stirred his pot. He's been taking another look at the Archers, but it seems they've cleaned up their act. There have been no complaints since he investigated them more than a year ago. Since Regis died, in fact. What do you think about that?"

I stared at her. "That's too coincidental to be a coincidence. One minute they're screwing every customer that walks through the door, the next they're clean, no complains. The timing is... it's bizarre."

She smiled, took another spoonful of sundae, then turned the spoon upside down in her mouth and did something to it that made my toes curl. She said, "I like bizarre. Let's go home." And we did.

19

The following morning dawned ugly. The rain was coming down in sheets. I was up and about by six; Amanda lay like a dead dog, a very beautiful dead dog, with the sheets pulled up to her chin. I placed a cup of coffee beside her on the nightstand, smiling. I shook her. She stirred and rolled away, taking the covers with her and exposing a naked backside Venus herself would have been proud of.

"Hey." I shook her again. "Come on. Get up. Have coffee with me."

She groaned. "I sure as hell am going to replace you one of these days, Harry Starke. It's Saturday, for God's sake. Go away."

I sighed, and left her to it.

I went back into the kitchen, grabbed my own coffee, then went into the living room and hit the remote to pull back the drapes. Visibility was down to almost zero. The rain and wind had whipped what little I could see of the river into an undulating field of tiny waterspouts.

Dressed only in my boxers, I parked myself and my cup on the sofa and stared out over the water

I had only been there a couple of minutes when, without a word, Amanda came out and sat down beside me. All she had on was a T-shirt, several sizes too big for her. On the back was a picture of a Teddy Bear and the words "Hug Me." So I did. It was a nice moment, quiet but for the rain beating on the windows, which was hypnotic. Finally, I turned Amanda loose and went out into the kitchen to make breakfast. Kate had sent a text at some point during the night. She had the warrant and would pick me up at my office at nine.

We ate. I showered, dressed—black pants, black dress shirt, shoulder rig for the M&P9, black loafers, and a black leather blazer. Morbid? Sure, but that's how I like it. I was ready to leave by eight thirty, but Amanda was still on the sofa, a second cup of coffee in hand, staring out at the weather.

"Hey. I need to go."

She didn't reply. She simply turned up her face and smiled. I leaned over, kissed her lightly on the lips, and told her I'd be back as soon as I could. She nodded and turned again to stare out over the water.

The drive over the Thrasher Bridge was a nightmare. I had the wipers on high, but they had little effect on the torrent of water lashing the windshield, and it was no better when I pulled into the lot outside my office. Thank the Lord I'd had that automatic gate installed.

I didn't bother to get out of the car. I just sat and waited for Kate to arrive. I only had to wait a couple minutes. The weather decided which car we would use, since there was no way she was going to get out of hers in the downpour, so I had to. "Equality for women" hah! Only when it's convenient, or the sun's shining.

We didn't have far to go, and we arrived at the Broad Street branch of the First Appalachian Bank only a few minutes later. The rain had not let up one wit. Fortunately, Kate was in a cruiser, so she parked in the rear lot close to the entrance.

The manager was a lady, perhaps fifty years old, very efficient. She took the warrant and stared at it, unsure of what to do. I had the feeling it was a first for her. She looked up and down at Kate at least a dozen times while she read every word, like some great black bird pecking for worms. Finally, she nodded, went to her desk, grabbed a set of keys from her desk, and asked us to follow her into the vault.

We both put on latex gloves while the old bird opened the box. She withdrew the inner container, placed it on the table, and turned to leave.

Kate stopped her. "I'll need you to stay and observe, Ma'am, if you don't mind."

The woman, silent, nodded. She stayed.

The contents of the box included only a letter addressed to "Whom it May Concern," a thick sheaf of copy papers, an envelope with a tiny, MemoQ digital recorder inside, and another with an SD camera card.

I wanted to get my hands on it all right there and then, but I knew it was impossible. The contents were evidence, and as such were subject to the chain of custody. They had to be labeled, documented, and sent to the crime lab for examination.

Kate placed each of the items in separate evidence bags or envelopes, then signed them, and had the branch manager countersign them.

"What's the chance of getting copies made today?" I asked Kate.

"Pretty good. The paper we can copy back at head-quarters. Whatever's on the recorder and the memory card will need to be copied by a lab tech to ensure whatever's on them isn't damaged or erased. That might take a day or two, but I can probably talk Mike Willis into doing a quickie. If not, we'll have to wait until the lab releases them."

"Sounds good," I said. "Let's get back to Amnicola and see what can be done."

We thanked the branch manager, then headed north. It was an equally short drive to the Police Services Center, and we arrived just as the lab people were leaving for an early lunch. We caught Mike Willis as he was heading out the door.

"Hey Mike," Kate said. "I need a favor. Can you spare us maybe thirty minutes?"

"Sure. What's up?"

Kate told him what she needed. He nodded, and took the two items from her. While we were waiting, she donned a pair of latex gloves, and made two sets of copies of the mass of paper and the letter. She'd barely finished when Willis reappeared. He'd copied the data from the SD card and the recorder onto DVDs: two sets, one for me, the other for Kate. I told him I owed him one, and then Kate drove me back to my office. I didn't go inside.

Instead, I climbed into the Maxima, called Amanda, and then headed home.

It was almost noon when I arrived, and the rain had subsided to a fine drizzle. Amanda had tidied up and prepared lunch. She'd cooked some tiny shrimp, iced them down, added mayo and alfalfa, and with a crusty baguette had made a plate of sandwiches.

I dropped the sheaf of papers and the two DVDs on the desk, and grabbed a bottle of Nierstiener from the cooler. We were all set.

I tried to let the copied evidence lie while we ate, but I couldn't do it. Halfway through I had to put my sandwich down and pick up the copy of the letter. It was from Angela. It was short, just a page and a half, but handwritten in cursive. Amanda had been sitting beside me, but when I opened the letter she got up, came around behind me, and read over my shoulder.

To Whom It May Concern,

I know it may sound melodramatic, but if you are reading this note I am probably dead.

It was exactly a year ago today that my husband Regis died. I was devastated. I was also convinced that his brother, Ralph, had had something to do with it. I still am. Dr. Gray said it was a heart attack. I didn't believe it, so I requested an autopsy. The result was the same, but deep in my heart I know he was murdered, and now I fear for my own life, but I will not give up trying to find out what happened to him. I know Ralph killed my husband, or that he paid someone else to do it.

Why did he kill him? Because Regis had found out that he, Ralph, was robbing the bank's customers. Regis had proof, of sorts—not enough to stand up in court, but enough to ruin Ralph if he exposed him.

In the box you'll find hard copies of counterfeit checks that Regis recovered from the company. They total several millions of dollars, all of it stolen. There's also a recording of a conversation between Regis and Ralph in which Regis accused him of the crimes, and there are photographs of Ralph with Ruth Archer. They were having an affair. Regis hired a private detective, a Mr. Solomon Wise, and had him follow Ralph. The man wasn't much good, but he did manage to get some compromising photos of the two of them together.

As you will see when you look at the hard copies, it appears that the stealing stopped when Regis died. I suspect that it continued, but with Regis dead and Ralph in control, I had no access to the bank records and so couldn't prove it.

Ralph is still seeing Ruth. I've seen them together myself on several occasions, and I suspect it may be her, or someone working for her, that is or was working with Ralph.

I can't prove that Regis was murdered, but I am convinced that he was. I think when you listen to the recording that you'll come to that conclusion too. I will not give up trying to find the proof, even though it may get me killed too. If that happens, I hope that you, whoever you are, will see that Regis gets the justice he deserves, and that Ralph and whoever he's working with get their just desserts.

Angela Hartwell
March 29, 2016

"Oh, my, God," Amanda said quietly. "That poor woman." She went back to her seat, picked up her glass, and took a big sip. "Oh, my, God," she repeated, leaning close to me, trying to see the letter. I read it again, quickly, and then passed it to her.

I knew Sol Wise. He was a weird little guy who ran a one-man private investigation agency out of an office on Rossville Boulevard. I wasn't sure how good he was, but I did know that he wasn't averse to skirting the law to get what he needed. He came to me for a job once, back when I first opened the office, and I probably would have given him one if he'd had the right qualifications, but he didn't.

He was cheap, and he didn't mind getting his hands dirty. From what I'd heard, he stayed busy, which must have meant something. I wondered what he'd found.

The letter hadn't told me much more than what I'd already learned from Dr. Gray and the Loftises. What I hadn't known was that Ralph was having an affair with Ruth Archer, and that put the entire investigation in a whole new light. For one thing, it would explain her keen interest in me and the investigation.

"Ralph Hartwell and Ruth Archer?" Amanda asked, her eyes wide in disbelief.

I shrugged. I was as surprised as she was. "Could it be true, I wonder? Was Ralph having it off with Ruth?

I guess we'll know in a minute."

I slipped the photo disk into the laptop and opened the file. There were two dozen photographs in it. Amanda watched as I brought the first one up on the screen. It was a little dark, taken at night with a medium telephoto lens, but the quality wasn't at all bad.

Good for you, Sol.

He'd chosen his spot well. The images had been shot in the country club parking lot, obviously from Wise's car window. The security lights provided good illumination, if weird coloring, but no matter; they were good enough to show to a jury. The first image showed Ruth and Ralph walking down the front entrance steps. From there, the shots progressed until they reached what I assumed must have been Ruth's car, a new, white Mercedes-AMG GTS sports car. The final four shots showed them both looking around, evidently to see if anyone was watching. The last three images showed them with their arms wrapped around each other, kissing.

Oh boy, do I know how that feels. Stupid man. Out in the open, in the country club parking lot of all places.

I heaved a sigh. I almost felt sorry for him, especially as I began to wonder what else might be going on between them. Could Angela have been right? Was Ruth involved in the check scam with Ralph? It would make a lot of sense, and answer a lot of questions.

And if she was.... If they were.... Hmmm. We'll see, I guess.

I ejected the photo disk and set it to one side. On Monday I'd get Tim to make prints. I slipped the audio DVD into the drive. Mike Willis had made an mp3 of the recording. The metadata told me it had been made on March 23, 2015, six days before Regis died. It was just over twenty minutes long. I hit the play button, and we listened to it all the way through. When it was done, we listened to it again. This time I made notes of the highlights.

"Ralph, you stupid son of a bitch," it began. I assumed the voice was Regis Hartwell's. "I know what you've been up to. I know you've been stealing from our customers. Oh, don't look so shocked. You knew I'd find out, God damn it. Just how long did you think you could get away with it?"

"You crazy piece of shit." That must have been Ralph. "You're out of your goddamn mind. What the hell makes you think that?"

"These!" The shout was followed by the rustling of papers. "They're checks, Ralph. *Counterfeit* checks. All of them fraudulent. You've gone too far this time. You'll go to jail for this."

"I had nothing to *do* with them, you... you... *asshole*. Why *me*? Why the hell do you think it was *me*?"

"Because you're goddamn stupid. That's how I know. I have your bank statements. Every time one of these things hit, you made a cash deposit."

"How the *hell* did you get your hands on *those*? I don't *bank* here!"

"No, you don't, smartass. That's another reason I know what you were doing. Why wouldn't you use our own banks, unless you had something to hide?"

"How... did... you... get... them?"

"Archie is a friend of mine, that's how."

"That's *illegal*, you piece of *shit*," he yelled.

"So is stealing millions of dollars, you friggin' *jerk*."

"I *told* you. I didn't *do* it, and *you* don't have proof that I *did*. Those pieces of paper mean *nothing*."

The conversation continued on like that for a while, each one shouting at the other, Regis accusing, Ralph denying any wrongdoing, until finally:

"Ralph," Regis said. "I've been covering these thefts out of my own pocket for almost two years. It's over. There will be no more. Do you hear?"

Ralph didn't reply.

"I have an idea who you're working with, but I want to know from you, and I want your resignation. I want it today. If I don't get it, I'll turn all of this over to the police, along with my suspicions, and let them sort it out."

"Bullshit. You wouldn't dare. You do that, and it will screw up the sale. You don't want that, now do you, brother?"

"You're right. The scandal created when it gets out that my own brother has been robbing the bank's customers for years would, indeed, screw up the sale. But you know what? I. Don't. Care. I've had enough. I'm out almost $6 million. I'm not going to do it anymore."

"*You're* out? *You're* out? *Screw* you, Regis. When Father died, you got everything. All I got was a shitty job wiping your backside. You want me to go? Fine. Here's what I want. I want $2 million deposited in my account by Friday; that's four days from now, and I want a settlement, a pension for life of $300,000 a year with cost of living increases. I figure that's about what I should have gotten when Father died."

"That's not going to happen. I'll go $500,000 and $150,000 a year, but that's all. I'll give you fourteen days to think it over. If I don't have your agreement by the sixth of April, I'll hand this lot over to the police. Now get the hell out of here."

And there the recording ended.

By itself, it wasn't proof of anything, but when you factor in that Regis died just six days after the recording was made....

I looked at Amanda. I couldn't tell what she was thinking. I waited, but she didn't speak. She just poured more wine and sipped on it.

"No thoughts?" I asked finally.

For several seconds she stared unblinking down at the paperwork on the table then said, "I think it's pretty conclusive. Ralph killed his brother. Not much doubt about it. That recording proves nothing, though. Nothing that will stand up in court."

"You're right, of course. But if you take the date of the recording, and then the date when Regis died, and you add all the circumstantial stuff: Ralph's affair with Ruth, these checks," I picked them up, "it certainly looks bad, enough for Ralph, or someone paid by Ralph, to kill him. It's also enough to get Angela killed too. She was right to be scared for her life. I don't think there's any doubt. Ralph killed Regis, and probably Angela as well."

"What about the Archers?" Amanda asked.

"They're in it up to their necks, but we can't prove any of this. Here. Let's go through this pile and see what we have. Maybe we can make something out of it."

There were more than a hundred sheets of paper. The first sixteen were bank statements, Ralph Hartwell's, going back more than eighteen months, from February 2015 to July 2013. Dozens of deposits for varying sums from $2,000 to more than $25,000 were highlighted in yellow. They totaled more than $300,000.

The remaining hundred-odd pages represented a like number of accounts, each one at a different bank, some as far afield as Knoxville and Nashville. On each piece of paper were copies of either one, two or three checks—some even had four—and a bank statement. The statements were short, usually just three or four deposits and one withdrawal. None of the checks were made out for more than $25,000; some were for as little as $500. But the monetary value of all the checks combined was more than $5.8 million.

The checks were dated over a period of two years; the last was dated just two weeks before Regis died. It was written by someone supposedly representing ASI (Auto Seating Inc.) for $527 to a bogus company called Westwood Information Technologies. That account was still open. The fact that that final check was dated two weeks prior to Regis Hartwell's death, wasn't followed up with more checks, and was never closed, indicated that whoever was working the scam had suffered a setback that caused them to close up shop.

Interesting.

"Almost six million," Amanda said wearily. "And all of it fraudulent. But what does it mean to us?"

"Not a whole lot, at this point. It's all circumstantial. Together it looks damning, but it won't hold up. We'll never prove Ralph murdered his brother, and to prove he killed Angela we need a whole lot more than this. We need to tie him to her. I didn't tell you this, but Mike Willis found a partial print on Angela's watchband. If it's

Ralph's, it will help, but it still won't be enough. He was her close relative. He could have grabbed her wrist any time in the weeks or days prior to her death. There's a chance we'll get some DNA from the hair that was caught in the watchband clasp. If that's a match, we'll have him. That could only have been caught there close to the time of her death. Any earlier and she would surely have removed it."

She nodded thoughtfully. "So what's the next step?"

"First, on Monday I'll have Tim make copies of everything. Then I'll confront Ralph and Ruth. Separately, of course. I'll also have my staff visit each of these banks," I indicated the pile of paper, "question the staff, and have them pull their security disks. Hopefully they keep them for several years. If not, we're screwed. I want to know who opened and closed each one of the accounts. Fortunately, I have the weekend to think it all through and go over this stuff again. You want to help?"

She said she did, which pleased me to no end, because I wasn't looking forward to spending the weekend alone.

20

I'd thought about the contents of the box and not much else for the entire weekend. I'd talked about it with Amanda until she could stand it no more and had threatened to leave. She didn't, but I also didn't stop. I couldn't. It consumed me. A weekend never went by so slowly.

I was in the office early that Monday morning, even before Jacque. As soon as she came in, I handed her the papers and had her type up a list of the banks where the bogus accounts had been opened.

The rest of the crew ambled in over the next twenty minutes or so, and I handed off the paperwork to Margo with instructions to make copies for Bob, Heather, Leslie, and herself. The disks I handed to Tim, again with instructions to make copies, and to make three sets of prints, one of which I intended to drop in front of Ralph Hartwell. And then I waited.

At nine o'clock, I had them all assemble in the conference room. We were about to get very busy.

"Bob. What are you working on right now?"

Bob Ryan is my lead investigator. He's worked for me almost since day one, and I love him like a brother, and not just because he's saved my life on more than one occasion; the last time not more than three months ago when he gunned down Sal De Luca and his brother Paul. De Luca was about to chop off my right hand with a meat cleaver. I owe him big.

"I'm just about finished with the Jamison and Essex cases, and I was about to dive into the Montfort case for Mortimer and Hunt. Did you have something else in mind?"

Montfort was a heroin dealer soon to stand trial for murder. Mortimer and Hunt were his attorneys. As far as I could tell, it was open and shut. They'd found the murder weapon in Montfort's car, but he claimed it wasn't his, and that he was being framed.

Oh yeah. He was being framed all right. I met that nasty son of a bitch before and I have no doubt he's a guilty as a squirrel with a mouthful of nuts.

"Okay. What about the Essex case?"

He grinned, "Caught old man Essex with his pants down, literally. It wasn't what his wife thought, however. He was having an affair alright, but it was with a man. I have an appointment with Mrs. Essex tomorrow morning at nine-thirty. I'll deliver the pics, see if she needs anything else, then wrap it up and send her the bill."

"Good. How about you, Heather?"

Heather Stillwell is my other senior investigator, and has been working for me almost as long as Bob. An ex-cop and GBI (Georgia Bureau of Investigation) agent from

Atlanta, she was something of an enigma. The GBI had had her on the fast track, but something happened. She never would talk about it. I suspected it was because she... oh, never mind. It doesn't matter. Not here anyway.

"I'm still working on Webber and a half dozen other small accounts, but I have some time if you need me."

"I do. How about you, Leslie?"

Leslie is one of my two juniors. She usually handled routine skip searches, process serving, court and records office searches; the day-to-day drudgery that I couldn't afford to have senior staff involved in. Point being, I knew she could free herself up, and that what I was about to put into play would be a chance for her to show what she could do.

"Nothing I can't put off until tomorrow, Boss," she said with a grin.

I smiled, and then handed round the copies of the checks and the list of banks. "Okay, we're all on board then. Here's what I need: Bob, split this list of banks between you. It would probably be best to do it geographically. They're where the phony accounts were opened. Then I want you to go hit them all. It will take time. Many are outside the local area: Nashville, Knoxville, Birmingham, Atlanta, etc. I want to know who opened them. I doubt very much you'll get names—real names, that is—but you should be able to get descriptions and, if we're lucky, video footage from the security cameras. If we can get some recognizable faces, Tim may be able to match faces to names. I want results, and I want 'em quick, but do a thorough job. Don't skimp on expenses. Stay overnight where you have to, but keep in touch.

Jacque will be your coordinator, but if you need me, don't be afraid to call me direct. Any questions?"

There were none.

"Ronnie, I need you to go through all of the paperwork, see if you can figure out just what was going on. I'm pretty sure it's a version of the scam you described the other day. Tim, you do some digging. See what you can find about these bogus accounts. Okay. That's it. Go to it, people."

Back in my own office, I made several calls. The first was to Jack Bentley. I made an appointment to see him at ten that morning. Next I called Sol Wise. I hadn't seen him for a while, but when I told him who I was, you'd have thought I was a brother calling him. He told me he wasn't busy, and that I could drop by anytime during the day. There were two more people I wanted to see—Ralph Hartwell and Ruth Archer, maybe even the twins—but I figured an unexpected visit would work best.

Getting out of my office is never easy. There's always a mountain of chores that need my attention. I did what I could, then handed the rest off to Jacque to deal with.

21

Jack Bentley's Cadillac GMC dealership was on Lee Highway, not far from the junction with Highway 153. I arrived there just before ten and was immediately set upon by a very enthusiastic salesperson, a smartly dressed young woman who thought my Maxima was the finest ride she'd ever set eyes on, and that it would surely trade in at a good rate. I let her down gently. Then I asked where I could find her boss.

He must have been waiting for me, because the minute I stepped through the big glass doors he was there with his hand out, a huge smile on his face, asking if I wanted coffee.

"Please," I said, and shook his hand.

He was in shirtsleeves with gold links at his cuffs, a solid blue tie with matching gold clasp, and light gray pants. It was a casual but expensive look. He was tall, a little overweight--his neck was already showing signs of age. I figured he was probably in his late forties.

He took me up to his office on a mezzanine that overlooked the sales floor on the one side and the service department on the other. He liked to keep an eye on his business, did Jack Bentley.

"So, Mr. Starke. Take a load off," he waved a hand at the two plush guest chairs in front of his desk. "I understand you've already spoken to Grace. What can I do for you?"

"Well, I wanted to talk to you about the Archers. Your wife told me you know them quite well."

"Er... I wouldn't say that, exactly. I knew Ben Archer *too* well, but he's been dead for quite a while. I've met his daughters at the club on several occasions--Ruth, I think, is more like her father than the twins, but...."

"Your wife said you fired Mr. Archer. What was that about?"

"The usual. Caught him stealing parts. It happens."

"How well do you know them, the Archers?"

"Not well at all. I've met Ruth a couple of times, socially, at the club, and everyone knows the twins, of course...." He hesitated, then said, "I've always found Ruth to be something of an enigma."

"Why do you say that?"

He gave me a funny look, then said, "She tries very hard to be liked, but there's something about her that... well, I don't know what it is. Personally, I don't like the woman."

. . .

I nodded. "What do you know about their business?"

"Thanks Wendy," he said as a young lady walked through the door carrying cups on a tray. "Help yourself to creamer, sugar, sweetener, whatever," he said to me.

I took the offered cup from the tray, but declined the condiments. Bentley made a show of stirring his own coffee, then looked up at me.

"The Archer business," he said thoughtfully, and then lifted his cup and drank. Another pause. "Hmmm. How shall I put it? Let's say.... Let's say... they are very profitable, very competitive."

He leaned back in his chair, elbows on its arms, his cup cradled between his fingertips.

I waited for a moment, but he didn't seem inclined to say more. "And?"

He sighed. Then he leaned forward, set his cup on the desk in front of him, and said, "There's something strange going on there, Mr. Starke. I have a previously owned vehicle department here, but I can't compete with them.

They go to auctions and buy quality vehicles, sometimes high-end cars--BMWs, Mercedes, Lexus, yes, and Cadillacs and GMC Trucks--and they sell them off cheap, to whoever they like, good credit or bad, which they can do because they finance in-house. They charge exorbitant interest, and they don't hesitate to repossess. If a customer gets two payments behind, he or she can be sure of a visit from Burke and Hare."

"Burke and Hare?"

He smiled. "ARC. Archer Recovery Company. Their in-house repo team. Luthor Crabb and Max Tully. A couple of badasses. They've always reminded me of Burke and Hare, you know, they were body snatchers back in the 19th century." He smiled. "My own little private joke. But you don't want them after you, and that's a fact. From what I hear it's the same at the Archers' boat yard, and their rental properties. Two late payments and you're out on your ear, with a helping hand from Crabb and Tully. They keep the deposit and the vehicle and resell it again, same terms, and usually the same results. I've heard tell of cars being sold three or four times in a year; very profitable. Look, I know this kind of thing isn't unusual in the used car industry, but the volume... well."

"So what do you think they're up to?"

"I don't really know. Something, that's for sure. I can't compete with them in prices *or* financing. They must take in a lot of cash. They could be generating bogus car, boat, and real estate loans and rents.

"I know what their inventory must be, or *should be* costing them, but more often than not they sell their vehicles for less than cost. Same with boats, so I'm told."

"Where do they get their cars and trucks from, do you know?"

"That's a good question. Someone is attending the auctions on their behalf. I say that because never once have I ever seen any of them, the sisters or their staff, there. They are never short of stock, though, and it's all quality stuff. Beats me," he said, shaking his head.

"Your wife said that you think that they didn't come by their money honestly...."

"Hah, that's been talked about, both at home and by more than a few members at the club. It's all conjecture. No one knows. Ben Archer made some money in his day; that's true enough, I suppose. After Ben died, though, the three girls built the business from the ground up, with Ruth leading the charge. Who knows.... I wish I could be more help, but they are a tight-knit family. As I said, an enigma.

"

"Well," I said, getting to my feet, "you've given me something to think about. Thank you for being so helpful. I really appreciate it."

We shook hands, and I left him sitting at his desk, a somewhat bemused look on his face.

22

Sol Wise was eating his lunch--a Big Mac, fries, and a large soda--when I arrived at the dingy little one-story building on Rossville Boulevard. The outer door wasn't locked, so I knocked, opened the door, and walked on in. Dominating the room was a battered walnut desk that must have cost plenty when it was new. Sadly, that day was long gone. It was now occupied by the erstwhile Solomon Wise, Private Investigator--it said so on the front door.

If you met him in any other environment, you might have thought him a bank clerk. He was in his late forties, and wore his thinning, graying hair in a comb over. His tie and vest were obviously part of a three-piece suit. A pair of round, steel-framed glasses sat low upon his fat little nose; the eyes peering through them were enlarged out of proportion by the thick lenses. He rose and came around the desk to greet me, wiping his hands on a brown paper towel.

"Harry Starke. How the hell are ya?"

"Fine," I told him, as he moved one of the two chairs in front of his desk, maybe six inches, for me to sit down. I'd seen offices like his before. Everything about it was functional and inexpensive. The floor was linoleum; his chair, probably secondhand, was leather but showed signs of extensive use. The two file cabinets could have done with a lick of paint, and the.... Well, you get the idea.

"So, Harry," he said with a huge smile. "You come to offer me a job, or what?" He picked up the soda and sucked noisily on the straw.

"Er... or what, I think. I need to talk to you about some work you did for Angela Hartwell. Do you remember it?"

He looked at me over the Styrofoam cup. "Why do you want to know about that? She send you?"

"No, Sol. She didn't send me. She's dead. They fished her body out of the river more than a week ago. I'm surprised you haven't heard."

The look on his face was one of total shock. He shook his head, violently.

"I didn't... I never.... Shit! How? I don't watch TV; don't see too many people. She kill herself?"

"Why would you think that?"

"I dunno. She was in a bit of a state the last time I saw her. Must have been five or six weeks ago, I suppose. I did a little work for her; followed her brother-in-law for a while; took some photos. She paid well."

"Just what were her instructions, Sol?"

"She thought he was having an affair. He was, though how involved it was I don't know. I only managed to catch him kissing."

"Ruth Archer, right?"

"How'd you know that?"

"I have the photos. I didn't see a report from you with them, though. How come?"

"She didn't want one. She paid me in advance, a lump sum. She said she needed photos. That's all."

"Now you and me both know that that's not all there is to it, Sol. You followed him, right?"

He nodded. "Yeah. Like I said. She paid well. I put in a lot of hours. I was waiting for him when he left home in the mornings and I was on his tail till he closed the door at night."

"So what else did you see?"

"Not much. He was pretty clean. I was about to give up when they finally locked lips at the country club. Oh, he saw plenty of her in her office—he was there a lot—but I figured it was business. She also came to his bank a few times. They were friendly, but outside of the country club parking lot, I never saw anything inappropriate; that's not to say there wasn't something going on at her office, or his—I mean, they were there long enough. I just didn't see it."

"Do you think he might have made you?"

He laughed. "Come on, Harry. You and me, we're pros, right? You think a schlump like Ralph Hartwell could make me? Never happen."

I smiled. I believed him. Like I said, I would have hired him years ago if he'd had the qualifications I needed.

"So you followed him. What else did you see?"

"Look. I wrote up a report, just in case she changed

her mind. You can have it if it will help, but I don't think it will. Like I said, he was clean. Saw a lot of Archer, but nothing I could nail him for." He rose and retrieved a file from one of the cabinets, then handed me the contents: three sheets of a computer-generated report. I glanced through it. He was right. Just his hours, and a long list of places Ralph Hartwell had visited.

Okay. There's not much here. I wonder....

"Sol, do you mind if I keep this for a couple of days? Better yet, can you make me a copy?"

He could, and he did.

"You want to earn a few extra bucks?" I asked.

His face lit up. "Sure. What do you have in mind?"

I thought for a minute. "I'm not entirely sure, yet. I want you to follow Ruth Archer. I'd have my people do it, but I have a feeling I'm being watched...." I paused. That thought had just popped into my head out of the blue. If my chin had dropped, I wouldn't have been surprised. *Am I being watched?* I wondered.

I shook my head and smiled to myself.

"What?" Sol asked.

"Nothing. Look, I've been talking to Ruth, and the twins, and by now I'm sure they know at least some of my people. I just need you to follow her, for now, but there could be more. I need to think about it. If need be, could you find a couple more pairs of feet?"

"I know a couple ladies. I think you know them too; they said they worked for you some time ago, when you brought down Little Billy. I've used them a few times before myself: Heidi Streck and Selina Cruz?"

"Yeah. I know them. Make the call and have them stand by until I figure it out. In the meantime, here's what I want you to do."

I told him what I needed, then left him to it. It was almost two thirty and there were some things I needed to do, in a hurry.

23

As soon as I left Sol's office, I called Kate.

"Listen," I said, "I've just interviewed Jack Bentley and Sol Wise. I need to go back to the office. I need to talk to Ronnie, and I think you need to be there. We need to put some pressure on the major players."

"Now?"

"What better time. I need to get his thoughts, then we can figure out where we go from there."

It was just after a quarter to three that afternoon when I arrived back at the office. Kate was already there, waiting in her car; she got out and followed me into the building. Ronnie was in his cubicle. Jacque started to get up, but I pulled a face and shook my head. She dropped back into her seat, obviously not pleased. It couldn't be helped.

"Ronnie, my office please." I said as I walked past.

I dumped myself in behind my desk, and pulled a

fresh legal pad from the drawer. Kate and Ronnie took the two guest chairs.

"Okay, my friend," I said, looking at him expectantly. "We need something to work with. You've had time to look the paperwork from Angela's safe deposit box over. What are your thoughts?"

"Ralph had quite an operation going, but... well we're not actually talking about a whole lot of money, not when it's spread over several years. I have to wonder if we have it all. Who knows? Anyway, most of the target companies were hit at least twice, with at least twelve months between hits, and different bogus accounts were used each time. None of the bogus company accounts were open for more than six weeks: money in, money out, via several wire transfers, all less than $10,000, to an offshore account in St. Lucia—a little more than $5.8 million—and then they were closed. That's it. A very short trail ending, as far as I can tell, at the bank in St. Lucia. it's classic."

"So, what are our chances of getting the bank to cooperate?" I asked.

"Absolutely none. First, I doubt very much that the money stayed in St. Lucia for more than a few hours. Second, the island is listed in the top five most secretive offshore banking havens worldwide. It would take a request for information from a federal agency to get their attention, and even then they'd stonewall. It could take years."

"So that's a dead end, then." I said it more to myself that to Ronnie. "So how would they get the money back into the country?"

"It's easy enough. Remember how Little Billy Harper did it? He used a bunch of shell companies. The money would be wired out of St. Lucia and, via a circuitous route, end up in one of several shells, untraceable. It could be used for anything. : investments, buying inventory for a used car dealership, for instance, or boats, real estate, untraceable loans that are never paid back...."

"Yeah, Ronnie. I remember. I get the idea...."

"Yeah, but if it's the Archers that are doing it," he interrupted me, "they have the ideal setup to pull it off. Think about it. The used auto industry deals in a lot of cash, especially at their level: cash for deposits, cash for monthly payments, cash to buy their stock. Same for boats; more cash. The same for their rental properties. Most low income rents are paid in cash."

I looked at him, waiting for him to continue.

"Here's another thought," he said. "The shell companies invest in the Archer businesses, make loans to them. The money is used to buy inventory or real estate, all of which can be sold later, at a profit or a loss – it wouldn't matter which. The investments and loans would be the fruit of the crime, but untraceable. The resulting income from sales would be clean, laundered. It seems to me that the only legitimate business in the group - always supposing what I'm postulating is correct - is the finance company. It being financed entirely by the sale of cars, boats and real property.

. . .

"So you think the Archers are behind the check scam."

"I have no idea. You'd know that better than me."

I leaned back in my chair and stared up at the chandelier. He was right. I did know it. The problem was: I couldn't prove it. The pile of papers on the desk had given me the front end of the scam, but I needed to catch the Archers at the source.

"What I do know," he continued, "is that the Archers are running one of the most profitable group of small companies I've ever come across. In 2014 they declared a net profit of more than $6 million."

"So how come they are so profitable? Exactly how would it work once they have their hands on the money?"

"That is the easy part. From what I've learned, they are selling upward of 100 vehicles a month. Let's suppose you go to an auction and buy a car, or boat. You then hide it, in a garage or warehouse. Then, on paper only, you sell it for cash. Heck, you could even take a deposit and finance it, again on paper. You make two, maybe three, bogus payments, repo it, again on paper, and then take it out of hiding and bring it back to the lot. You've just laundered six or seven thousand dollars, and you still have the car. Think about it. It's possible that as many as fifty percent, maybe even more, of their sales are bogus.: $150,000 to $200,000 a month."

It made sense, but again, how did we prove it?

"I would also suggest you look at their rental properties. They declared ninety-eight percent occupancy in

2014. I don't believe it. Most run in the low to mid-seventies percentile. I'd be willing to bet they are declaring bogus renters. If they are, say fifty or sixty of them, at $800 to $1200 each, we're talking $50,000 to $75,000 a month in cash income, clean money. Between rentals, cars, and boats the take could be two, three, four million a year.

"How do I do it, Ronnie? How do I prove it?"

"Beats me. If they're good at what they do, they'll have covered their tracks so deep, no one could run it down. What you have here," he picked up the pile of paper and put it down again, "is just the front end of the scam. If you can't catch them at the source.... You somehow have to tie them either to the checks or the bogus bank accounts, or you have to somehow prove the bogus sales, if that's the way they're working it. And I bet they are."

He didn't need to complete the thought. I got it, and he knew it. The problem was, I needed to stir the pot, and I needed to stir it with a shovel, but how?

"Kate?" I asked. "Got any ideas?"

She did. So did I, but between the two of us we couldn't decide what to do first. Kate wanted to interview Ruth Archer; I wanted to haul Ralph in for questioning. In the end, we decided to sleep on it.

It was after five when she finally left to go home. I stayed a few minutes longer to catch up with Jacque on the day's problems, and then she went home too, leaving me to lock up. It wasn't until I'd pulled out of the lot and hit the button to close the gate that I noticed the silver Mazda 3 sitting fifty yards or so down Georgia behind me. And I wouldn't have seen it at all had its lights not come on in my rearview mirror as I pulled out into the street. Those automatic driving lights are a dead giveaway.

I cruised down Georgia for maybe a hundred yards, then turned left onto Eighth, then left again onto Houston. Sure enough, the Mazda followed me. I pulled over to the curb and stopped. The Mazda accelerated as it went by me, but I got a glimpse of the man behind the wheel, a big guy almost too large for such a small car.

I shook my head. It wasn't the first time I'd been followed, and it sure as hell wouldn't be the last. I wasn't particularly bothered by it, but it did start me thinking. But now wasn't the time. I put the thoughts out of my head, hit the Bluetooth and called Amanda. It was Monday, so she had the night off.

This time I cooked. Steaks on the Big Green Egg: a fillet for her, and a Porterhouse for me, both served with baked sweet potatoes and a green salad. To drink, a cool Riesling for her, and a Blue Moon for me, no orange slice. We ate on the patio outside, and listened to the river, and watched the last of the rose-tinted sky over Lookout Mountain. It should have been a night to remember, and it would have been, if I could have gotten Ralph Hartwell and Ruth Archer out of my head.

24

As soon as I got into the office the next morning, I called Kate.

"Okay," I said as soon as she picked up, before she even had the chance to really say hello, "I've come to the conclusion that we have enough on Ralph Hartwell to bring him in for questioning. What do you think?"

She thought for a moment, then said, "Let's do it. I'll grab a cruiser and come pick you up. You do realize that the minute he gets here, he'll lawyer up though, right?"

"That I do, but before Donald Duck gets there, we'll have time to put the fear of God into him. He didn't strike me as being very tough. Even if we get nothing, we'll be able to read him, get an idea if we're on the right track."

While I was waiting for Kate, I called Sol Wise.

"Hey, Sol. Did you manage to line up your two investigators? You did. That's good. Here's what I want you to do. The Archer Real Estate Company owns 263 rental units; you can get the details from the records office. I want to know exactly how many of them are occupied, and how many are vacant. Have your ladies go and knock on doors. If no one answers, they are to get inside and look to see if the unit is vacant. I want a detailed list, and I want it yesterday. Capiche?"

He said he would get right on it and have an answer for me before the close of business. *Now that's what I like to hear.*

S he arrived at my office some fifteen minutes later. I'd already called ahead to find out where Ralph was.

His office was at the bank's main branch on Broad Street. He was actually talking to someone in the lobby when we walked in. He saw us immediately and, with a smile, turned to greet us. The smile lasted no more than a couple of seconds.

"Good morning, Mr. Hartwell," Kate said, also smiling. "We have a few more questions for you. I'd like you to accompany us to the Police Services Center on Amnicola. It shouldn't take long."

"Why—what, what for?" He was stuttering.

"Just a few questions. Nothing more than that."

"Why can't you ask them here? We can go to my office—"

"No, sir," she said, grimly. Both her smile and Ralph's had disappeared. "At the police department, if you don't mind."

"But I do mind. I mind very much."

"We can do it the easy way, or the hard way. Your choice. Either way, you're coming with us."

He nodded. "Give me a minute." He walked back into the bank, to what I presumed must be his private office. It was more than a minute. In fact, we were just about to go looking for him when he came back along the corridor, a somewhat sardonic smile on his face.

"I guess he called Donald," I whispered to Kate out of the corner of my mouth. She nodded.

"Am I under arrest?" he asked.

"Of course not," Kate said. "What on earth gave you that idea?"

He didn't answer. He walked quickly past us, out into the street, and stood beside the cruiser, waiting. Kate opened the rear door for him, placed the obligatory hand on to the top of his head, and closed the door, effectively locking him in.

As I expected, Daniel Drake, defense attorney extraordinaire, was waiting at the front entrance to the Police Department when we went in. He didn't look happy.

"What is the meaning of this outrage, Lieutenant? Why did you have to drag my client down here in a cruiser? You are damaging his reputation, and I won't put up with it."

I stood back a little and watched Kate tear him down —gently, of course.

"Mr. Duck," she said, and then quickly corrected herself. "Whoops, sorry. Drake. I haven't dragged him anywhere. He came of his own free will. And how can I damage a reputation he doesn't have?" It was said sweetly, with a smile, but I could see Drake understood Kate wasn't one to be intimidated.

"Now, Mr. Hartwell," she said, taking him by the elbow. "This will not take long. Your attorney is welcome to sit in while we ask you a few questions. I'll get you out of here just as soon as I can, I promise."

"We?" Drake said. "Does that mean you're including this... this... I don't know what the hell he is. If so, I strongly object. He has no right to question my client."

"Hmmm. How shall I answer that?" Kate said, still sweetly. "Yes, I'm including Mr. Starke. He is not a police officer but he *is* officially involved in this investigation, at my invitation and with the full support of Chief Johnston. So, if you wish to register your complaint, I suggest you do so with the Chief. In the meantime, I'm on a tight schedule, and you're wasting my time." And with that she turned her back on him, and escorted Ralph Hartwell into the building. I grinned at Drake. He glared back at me, his face white with anger.

The interview rooms at any PD are not designed to make the interviewee comfortable. Just the opposite. And the one Kate chose for this confrontation was about as austere as they come: a steel table, bolted to the floor. Steel chairs for the subject and representative on one side, also bolted to the floor, and steel chairs for us on the other. A video camera gazed down at the table from the corner opposite the subject.

As I sat I had a sudden feeling, not for the first time, that I was about to embark on a four-handed game of chess. It was a feeling I'd first experienced when I made detective more than thirteen years ago. Now, as then, it was game on, and the stakes were high.

Kate read him his rights for the camera, and Drake made the first move.

"My client will not be answering any of your questions unless I approve," he said.

"That won't be a problem," she replied amiably. "As you have decided on an adversarial approach to this interview, I will simply lay out some facts for you, and you, Mr. Hartwell, may comment or not. Let's begin, shall we?"

Drake nodded; Hartwell stared stoically at her.

"Mr. Hartwell," she said. "We have evidence that someone at Hartwell Community Bank was, until your brother died, stealing money from its clients, and that evidence points to you as the thief."

Way to go, Kate. Shock and awe.

I watched Hartwell's face as she said it. The muscles around the corners of his mouth tightened. He didn't answer, but Drake did.

"If you have such evidence, we'd like to see it."

She opened the file on the desk in front of her and took out a single sheet of paper. On it were copies of four checks, all seemingly written by one company to another. She handed it to Hartwell. He glanced at it, and passed it to Drake.

"As you can see," she continued. "Those are counterfeit checks totaling $30,873 written by ICT Manufacturing Inc. to a company called Askar Industrial Supply. The checks were deposited in a bogus Askar account at your Fort Oglethorpe Branch over a period of four weeks.

The fourth and final check was deposited on February 23, 2015. The entire balance was withdrawn via Internet banking two days later at nine o'clock in the morning on February 25, five minutes after the funds were available."

"So," Hartwell said. "The checks were counterfeit. We get a lot of those. What does that have to do with me?"

"Yes, you do indeed get a lot. In fact, over a period of two years, your banks have been hit more than 110 times that we know of. We recovered that information from a safe deposit box belonging to your deceased sister-in-law, Angela Hartwell."

Hartwell's eyes narrowed slightly; his lips tightened, but he said nothing.

"You asked what that had to do with you," Kate said, handing over a second sheet of paper. "That is a copy of one of your bank statements. You'll note several of the deposits are highlighted. Please look at the one dated February 26 for exactly $3,000, in cash. How do you explain that?"

He looked at the paper. It was shaking slightly in his hand.

"It's extra income. Nothing more."

"How do you explain that extra income, Mr. Hartwell?"

"It's easy enough. Back in the day, before Regis died, I had to do tax preparation to supplement my income. The son of a bitch kept a tight rein on his money."

"And you would, of course, have declared that extra income to the IRS?"

Now he was becoming angry. "Of course I declared

all of my income, including supplemental, to the IRS. What do you think I am?"

"I think you're a stupid little man, a crook that's not nearly as smart than you think you are. Over a period of almost two years you made similar deposits totaling more than $300,000. That's an awful lot of tax preparation. Why the hell didn't you just hide it under the bed?"

He didn't answer. More surprisingly, Drake was quiet too.

"You will, of course, be able to provide proof of where that income came from?"

Again, no answer.

"Fine," she said. "But before we move on, I should tell you that we have evidence of at least 100 more such bogus transactions and accounts."

His face was pale, his hands trembling, his eyes mere slits.

Kate smiled. "Moving right along. This was also found in Angela Hartwell's safe deposit box," she picked up a small digital recorder. She was about to turn it on but paused and looked up at him, smiling again.

"By the way, Mr. Hartwell," she said quietly. "Did you know that your sister-in-law thought that you murdered her husband?"

"You don't have to answer that," Drake snapped, and he didn't.

"Hmmm. I see," she flipped the play button on the recorder, and we watched the shock appear on their faces as the playback began. For twenty minutes we sat and listened as the angry conversation between Ralph Hartwell and his brother played out.

"Anything to say about that?" She asked when it finished.

Silence.

"No? Harry, do you have anything you'd like to say to Mr. Hartwell?

Before I could answer, Drake said, "He has no standing here and no right to say anything."

"Ah, but as I've already explained, Mr. Drake, you're wrong. Oh, before you get started, Harry, I'd like to show them both this." She opened the file, took out a photographic print, and passed it across to Hartwell. It was the final blow. I thought he was going to explode. It was of him and Ruth Archer wrapped around each other, lips locked.

I nodded, smiling. "You know what I think, Ralph? First, I think you killed Regis. That recording was made just five days before he died. Second, I think you probably killed Angela, too. We're just waiting for the results of a DNA test before we hang it on you. Third, I know without a shadow of a doubt that you were robbing Hartwell Banks, and that you were doing it in partnership with Ruth Archer."

"That's enough," Drake said, leaping up from his chair. "This interview is over. Come on, Ralph. We're getting out of here." Ralph began to rise to his feet.

"Sit down," Kate said, quietly. "Both of you. If you don't. I'll charge you with bank robbery right now, Mr. Hartwell. I have more than enough probable cause."

"You wouldn't be able to make it stick," Drake said. "That—" he waved his hand at the file, photo, and recorder—"is all circumstantial. It all can be explained."

"Perhaps it can, but it's definitely enough to charge him, and then I can hold him while I take my time proving Murder One. So *sit!*"

They sat.

"Harry," Kate said. "You want to continue?"

"As I said, I think you killed your brother. You had every motive in the book. First and foremost was your fear of exposure. Even if Regis didn't report the robberies, the sale of the bank certainly would have exposed them. Revenge would be a second motive. You hated your brother. He inherited everything, you got nothing, and you said yourself he kept you poor. Greed? You wanted it all for yourself. As to means, that was easy enough if you know the right people, and you certainly do. What did you use? Potassium chloride? Succinylcholine chloride? Either one would induce a heart attack."

I watched his eyes as I named the drugs. The first got no reaction. The second got a slight twitch of the eye. If I hadn't been looking for it, I would have missed it.

"You can't prove any of that," he said, but his voice cracked as he said it. He cleared his throat a few times, making kind of a big deal about it.

"Can I have some water?"

I got up, fetched a bottle, and handed it to him.

I watched as he drank, then said, "I know you killed him, Ralph," I said when he'd finished. We've asked for an exhumation order. If he had elevated levels of potassium chloride, you're toast."

It was a bluff, but Ralph couldn't help himself. "That won't prove anything," he snarled.

Drake grabbed his arm. "Shut up."

Ralph shook his hand off. "Potassium chloride is produced naturally in the body."

"That it is," I said, smiling at him. "So that's what you used, not SUX?"

This time he didn't answer.

"What about Angela?" I asked.

"What about her?"

"Did you do that, or did Ruth?"

"Piss off, you tin-pot shamus."

I laughed out loud. That was a first. I'd never been called a shamus before. I loved it. Unfortunately, he was right. We had a bunch of circumstantial evidence, but it was going to take more if we were going to take it to the DA.

"You want to tell us about it?" Kate asked. "It will go easier for you if you do."

"Screw you, lady. I didn't kill Regis; I didn't kill Angela, and I didn't steal from the bank. The only thing I'm guilty of is a drunken kiss in the parking lot at the country club. You can't even prove I was having an affair."

"Okay," Kate said, rising to her feet. "That will do it for today. You can go, but please stay close. I wouldn't want to have to come looking for you."

"You're not going to charge him with anything?" Drake asked. I think he was slightly perplexed at the idea.

"Nah," she said. "Not today, anyway. Plenty of time, eh, Harry?"

We walked them to the front entrance, and they left together in Drake's BMW.

"So," Kate said, turning toward me. "What did you make of that?"

"Not absolutely sure. He was robbing the bank; there's no doubt about that. I think he killed his brother, but he's right: that one is long gone. We'd never prove it, not unless we did exhume the body. He's right about the potassium chloride, but that's not what he used. He used SUX. I could see it in his eyes, and he's feeling pretty good about it. Up until a few months ago there wasn't a tox screen that could find it; it was untraceable. And he knows that. Now, though, so I've heard, there's a company in Europe that *can* find it, even if the body is fully decomposed. It would be expensive, but it's a thought. Maybe a last resort. And as for Angela? He sure as hell had motive and opportunity for that one. He has no alibi. Any word on the print Willis found on the watchband?"

"No, but that bottle of water you handed to Ralph might provide us with a match. I had it taken from him as we left the interview room. If they match, we have him, and I'll arrest him. We should know within the next hour or so. Let's go over the road and grab a coffee while we wait."

We did, but it didn't. The print did not match those Mike Willis was able to lift from the water bottle. That didn't mean Ralph didn't kill her. It just meant we couldn't tie him to her, yet! So who the hell did the print belong to? *Damn!*

"Okay, so what's next?" Kate asked.

"I think we need to go visit Ruth Archer. How about tomorrow morning? You up for it?"

"Sorry, I can't. I have an interview; one of my other cases."

I nodded. "Okay. I'll do it. I need to get hold of Wise first, though. I'm hoping he'll have something for me I can use."

I looked at my watch. It was just after noon.

"You want to go get some lunch?"

She hesitated for a minute, then said, "Sure, but we'll need to take both cars. I have to get back here by two-thirty. Where shall we go?"

"How about the Boathouse. It's busy, but close. We'll go in your cruiser and you can drop me back here afterward."

When I arrived back at my office later that afternoon, Sol Wise was waiting for me. A huge grin on his face and a sheet of paper in his hand.

"Here you go," he said, handing it to me.

I glanced over it. It wasn't much, just a few type-written lines and some numbers.

"That didn't take long. How'd you manage it?"

We all pitched in. I did some, the girls did the rest. What you have there is accurate. We looked inside every unit, all 263 of them. There were a lot of vacancies, as you can see. I kinda enjoyed myself. It was a chance to hone my skills a little."

"What sort of skills?" I asked.

He grinned, but said nothing.

"I get it. Plausible deniability, right?"

He just tilted his head slightly to one side, and winked.

I shook my head and smiled to myself.

"You were going to follow Ruth Archer. I'm going to see her tomorrow. Anything I should know?"

"No. Not yet. I tagged along behind her last night. She left her office at four and went to the club. She had dinner there, a few drinks, and was home by ten. I spent today knocking on doors. You said you needed that," he nodded at the paper in my hand, "ASAP, so I thought I'd better make sure you had it."

"Stay on her. She's up to no good, and I want to know what it is."

25

Ruth Archer had an office on the top floor of the building that housed the Archer Finance company. It was a small, two-story structure on Market Street, just west of the Choo Choo.

Just inside and to the right of the front entrance was an open door. The calligraphy on the glass pane read:

ARC Inc.
Archer Recovery Company.

Inside and to the right of that, a large man sat behind a desk. And I mean he was a *big* man. Easily 350 pounds.

The guy in the Mazda 3? Could be. He's big enough.

"Yeah? Whadda ya want?" Goliath growled when I knocked on the door.

Oh this one was a treasure. His head sat square on his shoulders and his huge jowls spread sideways, turning his face into a giant pear with an untidy tuft of black hair on top. Fat lips, a fat squashed nose, and small, piggy eyes under huge black brows completed the picture.

"I'd like to see Ruth Archer."

"She 'spectin' ya?"

"No, but she'll see me. Please tell her Harry Starke is here."

"'Arry Starke, 'eh? I know's you." He looked me up and down, then said, "Y'ain't so much." He reached for the phone, and his entire body shook, from the huge jowls on down.

He punched a single number into the keypad, waited a moment, then said, "'E's 'ere."

So, the word is out. She is expecting me.

He dropped the handset back into the cradle and waved a fat hand in the same general direction that I'd come. "That way. Up the stairs on the right."

I nodded, and left him staring after me. *Burke or Hare?* I wondered.

She was waiting for me. If she'd dressed to impress me, she'd done one hell of a job. For the first time in my life, I felt small. She was wearing heels that pushed her to an astonishing six foot five, and almost filled the damn doorway.

You had to be there. She looked like a runway model. The dark blue business skirt suit was tailored to accentuate her figure, and it did. She wore a white scoop neck under the suit jacket. I felt decidedly underdressed, and she knew it.

"You were expecting me," I said as she stepped back to allow me into her office.

"I was. Please sit down." I sat in one of her two guest chairs—they looked a lot like mine—and she turned the other chair so that it faced me, then sat down too. She smiled at me, and crossed her legs, offering me an unrestricted view of just about everything. Over the years, I'd been presented with similar views many times. I've never gotten used to it.

"Ralph called me. He said you'd been to see him and that you thought he was having an affair with me."

Straight to the point. No small talk, nice to see you, how are you?

I could do that too.

"Were you?"

She shrugged, looked away. "I suppose you might call it that. We did get together once in a while." All of a sudden my head was filled with the mind-boggling image of this amazing, statuesque woman writhing about naked with a skinny little man less than half her size. I smiled.

"What?" she asked.

"Nothing I can tell you about," I said. "So you *were* having an affair with him?"

"If you say so."

"I don't say so; I know so. I have the proof. "

"A couple of photos? I hardly think that's proof. As Ralph told you, they were the result of a little too much to drink and Ralph stepping outside his neat little box. No more than that."

"Oh, I think it's much more than that. In fact, I think

you two are up to your necks together in a whole host of dirty deeds."

She sat back in her chair, dropped her chin, and stared at me through her eyelashes. It was a look she'd given me before—right before she kissed me.

"What makes you say that?" she asked.

"Several things, not the least of which is that you seem to be very interested in the investigation into Angela Hartwell's death. In fact, the other day on the golf course, I got the distinct impression that you were pumping me for information. Why was that?"

"Because I was pumping you for information. But not for the reason you seem to think. I was doing it to get your attention."

"You already had that. What else were you after?"

She took a deep breath. "Why do you think, Harry? Why do you think I kissed you? I'm attracted to you, dammit."

I don't believe it.

"I don't think so," I said. "I think you know who killed Angela Hartwell. I think it might even have been you, or maybe one of your sisters. You saw her that night, at the club. What was that about?"

Her face had gone pale, her lips drawn tight, eyes narrowed. "She was leaving. I caught up with her in the lobby. I asked her to stop badmouthing me and my sisters, but she wouldn't talk to me. That's it. That's all there was to it. I wasn't the last one to see her alive; whoever killed her was."

"We know Ralph killed his brother. We also know he

was systematically robbing the Hartwell banks. I think you were involved with him in that enterprise. I can't prove it right now, but I will. You can bank on that, pun intended. I also think Angela was onto you both. You were, as far as I know, the last one to see her alive. I think she was about to expose you. She had to be stopped, right?"

"You're out of your mind, Harry. I have no idea what Angela was up to. She was always spouting off about her husband and how she thought he'd been murdered. You do know that she was a very troubled woman, don't you? And why on earth would I rob banks? I run four very successful businesses. I make more money than I can spend, than my sisters can spend, and that's a hell of a lot. I'll tell you this, Harry: you spread one word of these accusations outside of this office, and I'll sue you for slander."

I almost laughed at her, but the look on her face was anything but funny.

"Why would you rob banks?" I repeated back to her. "I think you did it because you could. I think it was a power trip, a way for you to look down on the little people and laugh. I also think it's in your genes. They tell me your dear old dad wasn't above stiffing people whenever he could."

"You... you—you son of a bitch. Don't you dare talk about my father like that. He—he, he was a good man, good to me, good to my sisters."

"Maybe, maybe not. But you, my dear, are a shark. A very beautiful shark, but a shark nonetheless. Ralph's a

guppy, but between the pair of you you've robbed
Hartwell Banks of more than $5 million dollars. Ralph
murdered his brother along the way, and you or one of
your sisters murdered Angela. And I'm going to put you
away for it."

"You're crazy," she said. "What the hell I ever saw in
you...."

"A dope. Or at least you thought you did. You're an
arrogant, self-absorbed egotist, Ruth. You think you're
smarter than everybody else. Well how about I show you
just how smart you're not?"

She glowered at me, but didn't answer. She still
wanted to know what I knew. Well, I didn't mind telling
her.

"I know you and Hartwell are robbing the banks. I
also know how you're laundering the money. You send it
to offshore accounts. From there it goes to shell companies that either invest the money in Archer or make
nonreturnable loans to the company, and then you wash
it, the money. I know every which way you do it. It's a
long list, so for now I'll just tell you about one of them.

"Archer Realty owns 263 rental units spread all
over Chattanooga. In 2014 the company declared a
ninety-eight percent occupancy rate. That's so far out of
the norm that I had it checked out. You know what we
found? As of yesterday afternoon, of the 263 units, 119
were vacant. That's forty-five percent. So the true occupancy is about fifty-five percent. You're washing money
through bogus rentals, more than 100 of them to the
tune of more than $100,000 a month. I also know
you're doing the same with the other companies in the

group: bogus car and boat sales, bogus... whoa, look at you."

The look she was giving me was one of such blind hatred I thought she might throw herself at me. If I'd thought she was capable of killing Angela before, I was sure of it now.

"Okay. Let's talk some more about Ralph for a minute, shall we? He's a nasty little piece of work, with less of a spine than a jellyfish. You do know that he'll bring you down, right? Hah, You don't believe me? Okay. Let's think about it. He knows we're onto him, both for the death of his brother and the loss of the $5 million from Hartwell's customers. You should have seen his face when I told him we were going to exhume his brother's body."

Now that really got her attention.

"He almost wet himself when we pulled him in for questioning. Just how long do you think it will be before he caves and gives up his accomplices? I'll tell you how long. The next time I put the screws to him, he'll break. If he thinks he can cut a deal and avoid prison by throwing you under the bus, he will."

She uncrossed her legs; no view this time. Then she walked around the desk, sat down, reached over and punched a number into the intercom, "Max. If you wouldn't mind. Please come in here."

A few seconds later, the door opened and in walked what I supposed could only be described as the Terminator. Max Tully was about as tall as me, but there the similarity ended. He must have weighed at least 250 pounds, but his body fat index was probably less than five percent. He was a body builder, a powerhouse, probably on steroids. He was so muscled his arms wouldn't hang by his sides.

"Mr. Starke is leaving now, Max," Ruth said. "Please show him out."

I stayed where I was. "I have a few more questions, if you don't mind," I said, reasonably.

"I do mind. Max?"

He took a step toward me. "You heard the lady,"

"Back off, Fatso," I said, even more reasonably than before, I thought, as I got to my feet and turned to face him. "Fatso," probably wasn't what I should have called him, but I learned a long time ago that the best way to handle a tough guy was to throw him off his game before he got started. Anyway, he went for it. He growled, and took another step forward. I took a step backward.

"I said, back off."

He grinned, exposing a set of white but crooked teeth, and raised his right hand to grab my shoulder. That's the trouble with big strong guys like him. They think their size and strength are all they need. This one, by the self-satisfied look on his face also thought he was better than me.

Fat chance, Blutto.

He didn't even see it coming. I made like the Flash, grabbed two of his outstretched fingers—the pinky and the one next to it—and bent them back. He howled in pain. His knees bent. His arm crooked upward toward his shoulder. His eyes closed. His head went back. Ruth sat staring, wide-eyed and open-mouthed.

"Down, boy," I said, as I slowly forced him to his

knees. I sighed dramatically, and increased the pressure until he was down on his back.

"All you had to do was ask nicely, and I would have left," I said quietly. "You didn't need to bring in the heavy —and that's all he is, Ruth: heavy."

I pulled on Max's fingers and he rose into sitting position. I bent down, put my mouth close to his ear.

"Max, I'll say this just once, so listen up. I'm going to let you go now. When I do, you'll stand up and go back to whatever hole in the wall you crawled out of. If you don't —if you decide you think you can ambush me—I'll blow away one of your kneecaps. I'll put you on sticks for the rest of your days. Understand?"

He nodded. He was in too much pain to even speak. I let him go and stepped back, and pushed my jacket back to expose the grip of the MP9 under my left arm. He got up and staggered out of the office, his right hand clasped in his left, close to his chest.

"Now." I turned to Ruth. "I will want to talk to the twins, but in the meantime I suggest you think about what I've said. It's better you come clean, rather than let Ralph do it for you. I'll leave now. Oh, and it's better you don't give Fat Luther downstairs any ideas. I don't want to have to hurt him too."

"Get out," she snarled in a voice so low I could barely hear it. Then she all but screamed, "*Get the hell out of my office!*"

I left. Her eyes were half-closed, two chips of flint filled with hate. The muscles in her face were tight; those in her neck were like steel cords. Suddenly she didn't look quite so beautiful anymore.

I went down the stairs, past the ARC office. The big guy was still at his desk, staring at me through the open door. His expression was unreadable, but I had a good idea of what was on his mind. I smiled and walked out into the late morning sunshine.

26

O n the whole I was quite pleased with the way the interview with Ruth Archer had gone, but afterward, as I sat in my car outside her office, I realized what little evidence I had of her or her sisters' involvement in anything: check fraud or murder. What I did have was all speculative. True, she now knew that I knew all about her crooked little operation, but unless I could tie them to some physical evidence I couldn't prove any of it. I needed more. I called Kate.

"You busy?" I asked when she picked up.

"That's a stupid question. Yeah, I'm busy. I'm always busy. But I'm glad you called. I have some news. Can you come by my office?"

"I can, but—"

"Get your ass over here, then. You'll be glad you did."

Click.

I looked at the phone, exasperated. I hit the starter button, put the car in gear, circled up onto I-24, and headed north to Fourth Street and from there to Riverfront

Parkway. Ten minutes later I dropped into a chair in front of Kate's desk. She had her seat tilted back, her fingers locked together behind her neck. She was grinning at me.

"So," she said. "How did it go?"

"Well, I managed to piss off a few people, including the redoubtable Burke—or maybe it was Hare. No matter. I got under Ruth's skin big time. I accused her of everything but robbing the cat of its dinner. She shrugged it all off, at first, but when I laid out her scam for her, and the probability that Ralph would cave and give her up, she lost it and called one of two repo men in to throw me out. You can guess how that went."

"So you think you got to her, then?"

"Oh I got to her. She's one thick-skinned lady, but at one point in the conversation she was coming apart at the seams. I wouldn't put it past her to do something stupid. I guess I'll need to start watching my back again." I grinned.

"Well," she said, "I have good news and bad news. The good news is, we finally got Angela's phone records from Apple. The bad news is, there's nothing there. Apparently she didn't set up the auto-backup feature. So all we have are her phone records from Verizon. No text messages; they only keep those for five days."

"Damn." I shook my head, then looked up at her. "Did she make any noteworthy calls?"

"See for yourself." She picked up a thick wad of printed pages and tossed them across the deck. "Those are her records for the last twelve months. There are hundreds of calls. To Ralph, her lawyers, friends—there are even a couple to Ruth Archer. It's a dead end, I'm afraid. Sorry."

I glanced through them, then set them on the edge of her desk.

"I'll have Tim take a look at them, but I'm betting you're right. What else?"

"We're still waiting on the DNA report on the hair follicle. I called earlier. Should have it by Friday."

"Hmmm. Well that's something, I suppose. What else?"

"Nothing. At least not now."

"But you told me to get over here, that I'd be glad I did. What was that about?"

She smiled. "I thought you might like to buy me lunch. Aren't you glad?"

"The hell I am. I was on my way back to the office." Actually, I *was* glad, but what the hell. She didn't need to know that.

We went to the Boathouse. It was just a couple of miles west on Riverside Drive. The weather was nice, a balmy seventy-two degrees, and we managed to get a table by the window. The view of the river was almost as good as the one from my Condo, and the food? As always, it was exceptional.

"You don't think she would, do you?" Kate asked as she nibbled on her fried calamari.

"Would what?"

"Do something stupid."

I sat back in my seat, dropped my spoon into the clam chowder, and thought about it. I'd learned a lot about people like Ruth Archer at Fairleigh Dickinson, but this was the first time I'd ever encountered one.

"She's a sociopath. Classic. So yeah. I think she might, especially if her back's against the wall, and right now that's just where it is."

Kate shook her head, "That's not good, Harry. One of these days you're going to push someone too hard, and they'll push back."

She was right, of course. I'd been pushing my luck for more years than I could count, but hey, what would life be without a little excitement?

"I wouldn't worry about it," I said. "I can handle her, and I can certainly handle her two goons." Then I had a thought. What if there were more of them—goons, that is? Then I had another thought. Amanda?

"Excuse me for a minute, will you, Kate. I need to make a quick call." I got up, walked outside, and punched the speed dial.

She picked up on the fifth ring, long after my heart had started to jackhammer in my chest.

"Hello, Harry. I didn't expect to hear from you until later this evening."

"What took you so long to answer the phone?" I demanded.

"Excuse me? What do you mean?"

"You usually answer on the first or second ring. I thought something might be wrong."

"I'd left the phone in the bathroom, silly. What could be...? Oh my God, Harry. Not again?"

Jeez, she's sharp.

"I dunno. Maybe. Look. I ran afoul of Ruth Archer

today. She's very angry. I think maybe angry enough to... well, you know."

"Damnit, Harry. Yes, I know. I know only too well. Last time you made someone angry, Jacque ended up in hospital for almost a month."

"Yeah, I know. It couldn't be helped this time. What time are you going in to work?"

"Three, as usual, and I'll be out at a quarter to midnight. Do we have to start this escort thing again? If so, I don't want to. You hear?"

"Yeah, I hear. I'll pick you up at a quarter to three. Pack Baby in your handbag, or whatever it is you carry these days." Baby is her Glock 26. I bought it for her and taught her how to use it during my altercation with Sal De Luca. She hadn't touched it, as far as I knew, since that mess ended almost six months ago.

She argued for another minute, halfheartedly, then finally gave in. I went back inside and finished my soup.

Am I being paranoid? I wondered. *Probably. But better that than the alternative.*

27

For what seemed like the first time in a couple of weeks I slept well that night. It had been almost midnight when I'd picked Amanda up from Channel 7. She was bushed and so was I. She was also more than a little concerned about the situation that had arisen between me and Ruth. She well remembered the five days in hell we'd spent back in January waiting for De Luca to show his hand. I didn't really think we were in that kind of danger, but... well, it just wasn't worth taking any risks. Ruth had struck me as being kind of... volatile. And then there were Tully and Crabb, her two heavies, to consider. So we talked for a short while, drank a half bottle of red, and then went to bed, and to sleep.

I arrived at my office early, busied myself catching up with some of the routine tasks Jacque had insisted I pay attention to and... well, it had turned out to be a pleasant and unusually quiet morning. I was sitting comfortably in my throne, a second cup of Italian Roast in hand, when my cell phone buzzed. It was Kate.

"Harry. It's me. I'm at Ralph Hartwell's house on Signal Mountain. You need to get up here, now. He's dead. Suicide. Doc Sheddon is already on his way. How long before you can get here?"

"What the hell happened?"

"You'll see when you get here. Get your ass in gear and come on."

I looked at my watch. It was just after eleven. From downtown it was a drive of maybe thirty-five minutes. "I'll be there by eleven-thirty. Don't let 'em move the body until I get there."

I made it in twenty-five minutes. Even the outside of the place was a madhouse. There were a half dozen cruisers, Doc Sheddon's official SUV, an ambulance, two fire trucks, and at least a couple of dozen onlookers standing at the roadside in front of the house. Kate was on the front steps. I hardly recognized her, covered as she was in white Tyvek.

She gestured to the officer at the gate to let me through.

"You're just in time," she said as I came up the drive. "Doc Sheddon is about to wrap things up. I asked him to wait for you."

"What does he have to say?" I asked.

"He'll tell you. Better cover up, Harry," she added, eyeing my shoes.

I grabbed a set of Tyvek covers from the box by the door and suited up, face mask, booties, and all.

Doc Sheddon was in the foyer. He'd already taken off his covers and was in the process of bagging them.

"Ah, Harry, m'boy," he said affably. "Nasty one, I

think you'll agree. But it's very interesting. Go on through. Take a look at him and then tell me what you see."

Ralph was in the library, just off the foyer, dressed in pajamas and seated in an easy chair in front of the TV. It was tuned to Fox News.

I stood for a moment just inside the room to get an overall view of the scene. Ralph was a mess. Blood had run from an entry wound at the right side of his temple and down onto his shoulder, where it had soaked through his shirt then pooled on the carpet below his chair. His chin rested on his chest. His left hand lay in his lap, palm down; his right elbow sat on the arm of the chair with his hand hanging over the end, palm up, fingers curled. Just to the right of the chair there was a small table. On the floor in front of it, below his hand, lay a Smith & Wesson 686 revolver. The grip looked clean, but there was blood spatter on the barrel and cylinder.

I made a wide circle around the body, taking care where I put my feet, even though they were covered. The exit wound on the left side rear of his head indicated a front to rear trajectory, just as I would have expected, and there was blood there. Hell, there was so much it looked like he'd bled out. Devastating as the wound was, maybe he hadn't died instantly. Finally, I completed the circle and stood and looked at the wound. It didn't look quite right to me. It was in the right place, front right temple, but I could see stippling around it, indicating that it wasn't quite a contact wound. The muzzle of the gun had been at least one, maybe two inches from his head. That was a problem, because the suicide's natural instinct is to press the muzzle of the gun against the skin.

I looked around at Doc Sheddon. He was standing with Kate in the foyer, just outside the room, still wearing booties. He was smiling one of those grim little creases that was always a dead giveaway: he wasn't at all happy.

"Come on, Harry," he said. "Out with it. Do you see what I see?"

"I dunno, Doc. Give me a few more minutes, yeah?"

I crouched and looked at the gun. There was something. I straightened, turned again to Sheddon.

"You have a pencil I can borrow for a minute?"

He smiled, nodding his approval, took one from his pocket and tossed it to me.

I crouched again, slipped the pencil into the barrel of the .357, and gently lifted it from the floor. As I did so, its weight swung it into the upright position, and I turned it so that I could see the grip. There were two minute spots of blood, barely discernable, on the back of the grip.

No way....

I looked at Ralph's right hand. There were two matching spots on the center of his palm, and several more on his fingers. I looked at the trigger. Nothing. Which was as it should be, but.... I laid the gun gently back where it had been.

"Harry?" His voice was low, almost mocking.

"Murder, Doc."

He nodded. "Tell me."

"The blood, if it is blood, on the grip. Transferred from the palm of his hand. There's not much, but there shouldn't be any. It's blowback. His hand was where it is now. It's not a contact wound either, hence the blowback and stippling. I think someone crept up on him while he was watching TV, shot him, put the gun in his hand so that his prints would be on it, and then let it drop where it is, thus the transfer. They were sloppy, Doc. I guarantee there will be no GSR on his right hand. Hell, even the position of his left hand is wrong. You don't sit there with one hand in your lap and shoot yourself with the other."

"It might surprise you to learn, Harry, that even today, not everyone watches CSI. But you're right, of course. I knew you'd spot it."

"Time of death?" I asked.

"Hmmm, hard to say with any accuracy. Probably sometime last night. Rigor is fully complete. It's quite warm inside the house, and even warmer outside, which will have affected the rate of the loss of body heat. The body temp indicates ten to twelve hours, but I think it's more likely twelve to fourteen. Lividity is fixed, so at least ten hours." He thought for a moment, his hand cupping his chin, stroking it, staring at me, unblinking. It was unnerving.

"Let's say nine o'clock last night, give or take an hour, shall we? I may be able to do better when I get him on the table. That's the best I can do for now."

He turned to Kate.

"Anything else, Lieutenant? No? Good. Well then. You two seem to have a handle on things, so, I'll leave you to it. Oh, I'll do him tomorrow, after lunch. Shall we say two o'clock?" And with that, he picked up that oversize black case of his and shambled off, humming quietly to himself all the way to his car, the Tyvek booties dragging in the gravel of the driveway as he went. He set the case in the SUV, spoke a word or two to the ambulance driver while waving his hands to emphasize his point, then he climbed into the car and drove away. The ambulance crew bagged the body and hauled it away to Doc Sheddon's lair.

I shudder to think about it. Hell, he could say any time he liked. I wasn't going to be there.

"So, Harry," Kate said, stripping off her covers and bagging them, "this really screws things up. Where the hell do we go from here?"

I looked at my watch. It was almost one o'clock. "Let's go somewhere and talk. I don't feel much like eating. Do you?"

She shook her head. "I couldn't eat anything, but a cup of black coffee sounds really good right now. But before we go, I want you to have a look at something." She held up a clear plastic evidence bag. Inside I could see an iPhone6 in one of those OtterBox cases.

"Ralph's?" I asked.

"Yup, and it was used to send a suicide text to his wife. All it said was, 'I'm sorry.' I called her. She's staying for a few days with her sister in Myrtle Beach. She ignored it. Thought he was apologizing for a row they'd had before she left. Thing is, if he didn't send it—and if he didn't kill himself, which he obviously didn't—somebody else must have, and that somebody was probably the killer. Which means it could give us an accurate time of death." She gestured for the lead CSI tech, and handed him the baggie.

"There's a McDonalds on Dayton Boulevard," I said. "That work?"

She nodded.

When it came down to it, I couldn't handle the thought of Mickey D's food either, so we settled for Lillie Mae's Place instead. At least they serve a decent cup of coffee.

We grabbed a table by the window, and as we sat I was struck by a wave of nostalgia. Kate and I, we'd done this so many times over the years. So many tables, just like this one. Hell, I missed it. I missed Kate. I could tell she knew what I was thinking, because she kept looking at me and then down into her coffee cup.

"You miss it too. Don't you?" I asked. Was that moisture in her eyes?

"You son of a bitch," she whispered. "Why did you have to screw it up?"

"I...." I had no answer. It had been totally my fault. I reached out and put my hand on hers, but she snatched it back.

"Don't do that. You made your choices. You have Amanda now. There's no going back. I just hope you don't do to her what you did to me."

"Kate, I—"

"Let it go, Harry. We need to talk about Ralph Hartwell."

I shook my head. I could have cut the atmosphere with a rusty knife. I got up. Fetched us both a second cup of coffee. Looked at her from across the room while I was getting it. Her eyes were red. I felt like shit.

Somehow, we got through the next few minutes and yet another cup of coffee, but it wasn't easy.

Finally: "Okay," she said. "He was murdered, and by someone who didn't know what he or she was doing. Who did it and why?"

"Who?" I asked. "I think It may have been my visit to Ruth yesterday that caused it. I laid it all out for her. Told her I knew she was in cahoots with Ralph, robbing the banks. I even suggested she killed Angela to stop her from exposing them. So, one or all of the Archers killed Ralph; has to be. Why? To stay out of jail."

"Easy for you to say," she said. "How the hell do we prove it?"

"The fact that Ralph is gone doesn't mean he didn't kill Regis, or Angela, for that matter. I think he probably did kill his brother. Angela? I don't know. If he did kill her, why did he cart her all the way to the golf course? It would have taken more than one person to get the body down the embankment to the river, so if he killed her, who helped him? Why would anyone do that?"

"So what makes you think it was the Archers?"

"Process of elimination. Look, they were obviously in bed together, literally and in crime. Ruth was screwing Ralph for sure. The Archers' business interests are borderline legal at best, downright criminal at worst."

"Yeah, but—"

"Okay. Answer me this: You've seen Ralph, alive and dead. He was an ugly little critter, not the sort to attract the likes of Ruth Archer. So what did she see in him?

Money. She saw lots of money. Ralph might have come up with the counterfeit check scheme. It's not new, and he would have known about it from his banking experience, but he sure as hell wasn't smart enough to carry it out. Ruth Archer was. Think about it. She's always there, somewhere. Either hovering in the background or right out front."

I looked at her. She was slowly shaking her head.

"Okay. I'll boil it down for you," I said. "One: we think Ralph killed Regis. Two: Ralph is having an affair with Ruth. Three: Ralph is stealing. Four: Ruth is a crook. Five: Ruth has been paying far too much interest in me and the investigation. Six: Someone is laundering the ill-gotten gains; I think that's Ruth. Seven: Ralph and Ruth are about to be exposed by Angela. Eight: Angela is murdered. Nine: We question Ralph. I question Ruth, and then Ralph is killed. I could go on." I spread my hands. "Kate, that's way too many coincidences."

She thought about it. I could almost see the wheels turning inside her head.

Suddenly, she seemed to make up her mind. She nodded, leaned back in her seat, and clasped her hands together in front of her. "Okay. I'll buy it. But how do we prove it?"

"First, we need to search his office," I said. "Maybe something interesting will turn up."

"I'll head that way as soon as we leave here."

"I also think we need to take a look at the Archer's vehicles. If Angela was killed or incapacitated somewhere other than at the club; in her apartment, for instance, she must have been moved. That means whoever did the moving must have used a vehicle. It couldn't have been Ruth's Merc; there wouldn't have been enough room. We need to find out what the twins drive. Or maybe Burke and Hare helped; let's grab their vehicles too."

"I can do that. It shouldn't take but a couple of minutes." She called her office and put in the request, and then we waited for the callback. It came in less than five minutes. Rachel had a Toyota Highlander. Rebekah owned a 2015 Jeep Grand Cherokee. The two repo men drove a recovery vehicle, a Ford 250 King Cab with a hydraulic lift.

It was after two o'clock when we got out of Lillie Mae's. Kate took me back to the PD, and I left her to make the arrangements necessary to seize the vehicles.

It didn't take long.

I was in my car and just turning into the office lot when Kate called to say that the warrants had been issued and three teams of officers had been dispatched. The vehicles would be seized and transported to the CSI compound.

Like with the DNA match, it would be a couple of days before we had a definitive answer.

28

The obligatory Friday morning staff meeting ended around nine-thirty. The attention I gave the office's minutia hadn't been what it could be, and I was antsy to get out of there.

As soon as I made it into my own office, I grabbed my phone and called Kate.

"Hey. It's me," I said. "Listen. I've been thinking—"

"Did it hurt?"

"What? No. Dammit, Kate. Be serious. I was thinking. Angela Hartwell said in her goodbye letter that, even though the stealing seemed to stop when Regis died, she suspected that it had continued."

"And that matters because...?"

"Because if it did continue, Ralph probably kept records. If so, where are they? Have CSI finished with Ralph Hartwell's home yet? Did they find anything?"

"I haven't heard. It's a bit soon, but hang on a minute and I'll check."

The wait seemed interminable.

Kate came back on the line. "They found some interesting traces—nothing they're ready to talk about yet—but they didn't find any interesting papers."

"You searched his office at the main branch, right?"

"Yesterday afternoon, yeah, but it was clean. I don't think the man did a whole lot of work there. It was a typical executive suite, all show and no dough."

I'd figured as much. "Okay, I think we need to talk to Mary Hartwell. I'll set it up. I'll need you to be there with a search warrant."

"I can do that. What are we looking for?"

"Keys. Specifically, safe deposit box keys. It makes sense that Ralph wouldn't keep secret papers at the office, but nor would he bury them in the backyard. He'd keep them in a bank. Maybe at one of his own branches, but more likely at another bank entirely. Now, where would he hide the key? If he's smart, he'd know the best place to hide a small item would be in plain sight."

"Makes sense. Give me a couple of hours. I'll call you." She disconnected before I could answer.

Damn. I'm gonna have to talk to her about her telephone etiquette.

I called Mary Hartwell and asked for an early afternoon appointment. She reluctantly suggested three-thirty; I suggested two o'clock. I won.

It was a different Mary Hartwell that met us at the front door. She must have been to the salon, because her hair had been cut and colored. It was still blonde, but much darker and now with highlights. Her clothes were expensive, stylish, more suited for business than pleasure. If this lady was in mourning, she certainly didn't show it.

"I hope this is not going to take long," she said as she stood stiffly back to allow us to enter. "What exactly do you want to talk to me about?"

"I have a warrant to search the house," Kate said and handed the papers to her.

"It's already been searched, and thoroughly, by your forensic people. I thought they were done."

"They were, but something's come up. So, if you please. We'll begin with Mr. Hartwell's office."

"If you'll tell me what it is that you're looking for, maybe I can help," she said, leading the way through to what I assumed was an extension at the back of the house. Neither Kate nor I answered.

It was an office, that was for sure, and obviously the place where he'd spent a lot of time. Cluttered, untidy, papers, books, photographs, two computers, printer, router—the list went on.

I sighed.

She heard it. "As I said," she repeated, "perhaps I can help."

"We're looking for proof that Ralph was still robbing the bank's customers. That would be record books, accounts, but more likely it would be a key to a safety deposit box."

I turned and looked at her. She wouldn't meet my eye.

"You know. Don't you?" I asked.

She didn't answer. She sighed, shook her head, and walked out of the room. She returned a moment later with her handbag. She reached inside, rummaged around the bottom, withdrew a key ring with three keys on it, and handed it to me.

"There's a safe deposit box at the main downtown branch. I'm running things now. I can get you in. I've looked in it, by the way. It contained only life insurance papers and other personal documents." She paused, and then continued. "Look, you have it all wrong. Ralph stopped all that when Regis died. It scared him, and he didn't have the stomach, or the balls, to continue whatever it was he was up to. Honestly."

Honestly? Hmmm.

I handed the keys to Kate. "We'll need a warrant to open it," she said. "If not, any evidence we might find in it would be the product of an illegal search and wouldn't be admissible."

She nodded, "I understand. I told you what was in it, but you can rest assured that the box will not be disturbed again until you open it. When is that likely to be?"

Kate left me alone with her and went outside to make a call. She returned a moment later.

"I can pick it up in an hour. Can you meet me at the bank at say," she looked at her watch, "five o'clock?"

"Certainly. Now, if you've finished here...."

"Not quite. I've ordered the CSI team back to search the place again. No, no." She held up her hand as Mary was about to speak. "It's not that I don't believe you. I just need to satisfy myself that we haven't missed anything."

"She was lying through her teeth," Kate snarled as we drove back down Signal Mountain. "You can bet that whatever was in that box, and I'm certain there was something, is long gone. It's barely worth the time it will take to go look at it, but I have to. Damn!"

I smiled to myself, then gritted my teeth as she swung the car around the tight bends of the mountain road. Next time, I'd drive myself. She was right, though, except for one thing: If we hadn't experienced the new Mrs. Hartwell, the afternoon would have been a complete waste of time. It sure as hell hadn't taken her long to take over the reins of the Hartwell banking empire. Mrs. Hartwell was now a very wealthy woman.

29

The following morning didn't start well. After arguing half the night with Amanda, I woke up late. I left her sleeping, grabbed a quick shower, and drove straight to Amnicola to meet with Kate and Mike Willis. He was already seated in her office, with a coffee cup in hand and a pile of paperwork on the edge of her desk. Kate, though lovely as ever, was in a rare, pissy mood. I could see that through the open office door. I wasn't feeling too chipper myself, and I was in no mood for what came next.

I knocked on the doorframe and stuck my head inside, but before I could say anything—

"About damn time. Where the hell have you been?"

Mike grinned up at me, and raised his cup in a mock toast. "Morning, Harry."

I looked at my watch. It was just after nine o'clock.

"Mike," I said with a nod. To Kate: "Who the hell kicked your cat?"

"I've been here for almost an hour. Mike's been here since eight thirty...."

"Whoa," I said. "Let's get something straight here. I don't work for you. Today is Saturday. I don't work weekends. Furthermore, you are not paying me for my time." The more I said, the angrier I became. I was about to lose it completely. "You dragged me into this mess and now you think you can treat me like one of your rookies. I left the force to get away from this kind of crap. Tell you what. Screw it. I'll come back when you're in a better mood."

I turned and walked back out of the office, leaving her staring after me, open-mouthed.

"Hey. You come back here." I ignored the shout and continued on, straight out the front entrance. I was opening the car door when she appeared on the steps behind me.

"What the hell is wrong with you?" she asked. "Damn, you can be a touchy son of a bitch."

I pulled the door open. "Yeah, I can, and I don't have to put up with your crap. I walked away from all that ten years ago."

"Okay, if that's the way you want it. I'm sorry I pissed you off, but I'm not going to beg. Have a nice day, Harry Starke."

I stood beside the open car door, staring after her as she walked away.

She really does have a nice ass.

I sighed, slammed the car door, and went back inside. I grabbed a cup of coffee from the machine and went back to Kate's office.

"Sorry," I said. "I guess I overreacted." I sat down in the chair next to Mike. They both looked at me; neither one of them spoke. "Okay," I said, unable to keep the edge out of my voice, "you want to get on with it, or not? You're on my time now, and I haven't got all day."

Kate simply looked at Willis and nodded. She picked up her cup, held it in both hands, and stared at me over the rim as she sipped.

"Um... alrighty then," Mike said, in a fair imitation of Jim Carrey. "I'll begin with the good stuff. We did a thorough search of the Hartwell home, both times, but we found almost nothing. There were prints everywhere, mostly they belonged to Mr. and Mrs. Hartwell. A few didn't, including yours, but they were all easily accounted for and eliminated. Ralph's phone had one of those armored glass screen protectors; it had been wiped. So had the case. So there was nothing there. But we did find something interesting. We had Rex George—he's the go-to man where blood spatter's concerned. We had him take a look at what we had, both on and around the body, and he found something. One of the splashes was a little different from what you'd expect, both in pattern and composition."

"Oh?" I said.

"Yeah. See, blood spatter from a close contact wound is usually high velocity. It flies fast and makes a distinctive pattern when it hits. This wasn't like that. It was more of a gob, a droplet. The direction of travel was different from the rest of the spatter. Instead of traveling away from the body to its right, it traveled across in front of it, from right side to left. It landed just beyond and in front of the left foot. It could not have come from the gunshot. That would have been impossible."

"So how did it get there, then?" Kate put her cup on the desk and leaned forward. "You're saying the blood isn't Hartwell's, right?"

"Oh, we're pretty sure it came from the victim, but not in the way you'd expect. It consisted of blood and minute fragments of brain matter and... saliva. I think maybe the killer had his mouth open when he pulled the trigger and got himself a mouthful—well, some at least—and then spat it out. That would account for the direction and pattern."

"Saliva? Are we talking about the killer?"

He nodded, "I think so. We took samples. I'll know for sure when we get the results of the DNA screen back from the lab, but that's going to take a while."

Damn! Why do these things always have to take so long?

"Well, that's something, I suppose," I said.

"Hey, don't be so pessimistic. If we get a solid DNA profile of the saliva, you can solve this thing, right?"

"It would help, that's for sure. Anything else?"

He shook his head. "Nope. Whoever killed him was very careful. No hairs, fibers, nothing other than the saliva. I guess we could call that a bonus, if it pans out."

"How about the hair?" I asked. "Nothing back from the lab yet, I suppose?"

"From the watch band? No. I'll give 'em a call when I get back to my office. See if I can chivvy 'em up a little. Now, on to the bad news. The Archer vehicles. Nothing. I had a team working on them until almost midnight on

Thursday and all day yesterday. They're clean. They hadn't been cleaned; we just didn't find anything. If they transported her, they didn't use those vehicles, which means that if they did move her... they must have used one of the vehicles off the lot. If you want them processed, it will take a couple of months."

I was tempted to ask him if he was sure, but I wouldn't insult the man. If he said it, it was fact, that was good enough for me.

"Okay." He looked at each of us in turn. "If that's all, I need to get back to the lab. We had a double in last night: murder-suicide."

He got up, picked up his pile of papers, and left. Kate tilted her chair back and stared at me. It wasn't pleasant.

"What?" I asked.

She merely shook her head, then stared up at the ceiling. "Harry, what the hell are we doing?"

"Doing? We're trying to solve a double homicide."

"No, that's not what I meant. I meant, what's happening to us? We never used to be this way with each other. Working together used to be fun. I loved it. Now? I don't know. I feel like... every time I talk to you, I'm bothering you somehow. Am I?"

Now I began to feel like a real ass.

"No. Absolutely not, but you're right... well, partly. Look, I had a tough night. Didn't sleep worth a damn. You just caught me on the wrong foot is all. My fault. I'm sorry. Let's put it behind us, okay?"

She nodded, but....

And then she seemed to brighten up.

"So," she said. "What are you thinking?"

"About the case? I think Ruth, and maybe her sisters are good for it, but we need a break. Maybe the saliva is it. Who knows?" We sat quietly, both of us thinking.

"Kate," I said at last, "we've been at this thing now for more than two weeks and have almost nothing but a few theories. It's going nowhere. Unless we get something back from the lab, it's dead in the water. I was pushing my luck when I accused Ruth. Unless we can somehow tie her to it, even the check scam is a nonstarter. The DA would throw it out. I need to get back to the office, see what the crew visiting the banks has come up with." I got up, looked down at her across the desk, "You okay?"

She nodded, but I could tell she wasn't.

30

The first thing I did when I got into the office Monday morning was call Sol Wise. I needed to know if his tailing Ruth Archer had produced any results. It hadn't. I told him to stay on it, and to put his two investigators on the repo men. Why I did that, I had no idea. It was just a feeling that I needed to know more about them, and I never ignore such feelings.

Next, I walked out into the bullpen to get coffee. Bob Ryan had just arrived.

"Harry," he said. "We need to talk. I may have something."

We both made ourselves coffee, and then went to my office. He put his cup on my desk and his briefcase next to it and, still standing, opened it and took out three DVDs. I sat down behind my desk. He placed the disks in front of me.

"What do you have, Bob?"

"Let's wait for Heather. I'm willing to bet she has exactly the same stuff I have."

I picked up the phone, buzzed Jacque and told her to send Heather in as soon as she arrived. The door opened almost immediately, and Heather walked in. She was grinning from ear to ear.

"You too?" Bob asked.

"I think so." She sat down in one of the guest chairs, opened her briefcase and retrieved two disks just like Bob's.

"Okay," I said. "Sit down, Bob. Let's hear it."

He sat, and looked at Heather. She shrugged.

"All women," he said. "Every one of the accounts I visited was opened by a woman." I made it through twenty-five banks and then called it quits. There was no point in going on. It was the same thing every time." He looked at Heather, his eyebrows raised questioningly.

"The same," she said. "I stopped after only twenty, I'm afraid, but when you look at the images, I think you'll see why. Right?" She was looking up at Bob.

"Absolutely. Not just women, one woman. Take a look." Heather stood and put her disks beside Bob's.

I slipped the first of the disks into the drive. There were literally hundreds of images on it. All were of women. All were from security camera footage. In some the women were walking into the bank, in some they were seated in front of the clerks' desks. At first I thought they were all different, but then I got it. It was the same woman, but in disguise, wearing different wigs, glasses, hairstyles, you name it. The metadata told me the images had been collected over a period of three months. I looked up at Heather, then at Bob. Both were smiling. Bob handed me another disk. It was the same. This time, though, the images had been taken over a different period. I started to laugh.

"What?" Bob asked.

"It would be funny if it weren't so stupid. Oh, none of them are recognizable as such, and there aren't many where the full face is visible from the front, but I know who it is—or rather, who they are."

"They?" he asked. "I thought they were the same person."

"Maybe, but I don't think so. I think it's the Archer twins."

They both looked at me, smiling.

"You're kidding, right?" Heather asked.

"Not at all. Unfortunately, I can't prove it. The disguises are good, and the girls look so much alike anyway."

I picked up the phone and punched the button for Tim's extension. "Can you come in here for a minute, please, Tim?"

"Here," I said when he arrived. "Take a look at these and tell me what you think?"

"Bank robber?" he asked.

"Er... yeah, at least I think so. I need to know who this woman is.... No. I already know that, but I need to know for sure. I need something I can use for proof. Can you do that?"

He looked at me quizzically.

"Okay. Sorry I asked. Of course you can. How and when?"

"If you know who it is, I need a photo, full face frontal, to use as a baseline. Do you have one?"

"Unfortunately, no. Bob?"

"I'll get one. Where do I go?"

"Fortunately, they're identical twins, so you only need to find one of them. I suggest the dealership. Rebekah Archer runs it."

"Okay. Let me get caught up here, and then I'll go. Anything else?"

"No. You did great. Both of you. This may be just what I needed." I turned to Tim. "How long?"

"Not sure. Once I have the photo, it will take a while for my facial recognition software to run the images. Unfortunately, mine's not as good as the FBI's, so it will take a while longer. Tomorrow, maybe?"

"As soon as you can."

31

I picked Amanda up from Channel Seven at the usual time that evening, just after a quarter to midnight, after the late night news broadcast. As usual, she was starving.

"I need food, Harry." *Damn! These late nights are killing me.*

"You always need food. How the hell you keep the pounds off is a mystery."

"No it isn't. I eat healthy and I work out, a lot."

I had to admit, she was right on both counts: she did work out—I loved to watch her—and she did eat healthy, most of the time.

"So feed me, then. Before I pass out."

"I have some Tilapia. We could have that with a green salad, yes?"

She nodded. "I could murder a plate of fries. Do you have those too?"

"Frozen, yeah."

"Goodie. Fish and chips and salad. Go, go, go. I told you, I'm starving." I went.

I parked the car in my garage and closed the door behind us. The first thing I did when we entered the living room was head for the drinks cabinet. I retrieved the half empty bottle of Laphroaig on instinct, then paused and looked at Amanda.

"I'll have wine, if you don't mind," she said, heading for the kitchen. As I watched her go, the summer dress swinging around her knees, I was once again struck by how lovely she was, no matter the angle of the view.

I poured myself a healthy three fingers of Scotland's best—ah... maybe it was four fingers. Amanda came out of the kitchen with a tumbler full of Nierstiener.

"That's uncouth," I said.

"Screw the couth," she said with a laugh. "I'm thirsty and, anyway, it'll save me a trip to the kitchen to get more."

"Oh I very much doubt that," I said, also laughing.

She leaned in close and kissed me on the lips. She tasted... amazing, a combination of cool white wine and cherry lipstick.

"So? Are you going to feed me or not?"

I sighed and got to my feet. "You are so high maintenance."

"But worth it, right?"

I had to admit it: she was.

I fixed the fish. It took only a few minutes, and then I fixed the salad, and threw a load of frozen crinkly fries into the oven. Ten minutes later, we were at the table enjoying the meal. Life was good.

The meal finished, Amanda stacked the plates in the sink and refilled her tumbler. I refreshed my glass of scotch, and we retired to the sofa in front of the window. I thumbed the remote to dim the lights, and we sat quietly together, looking out over the river. The water was still, the reflections of the moving lights on the Thrasher Bridge glittering on the surface. A three-quarter moon cast eerie shadows along the far bank almost 200 yards away. Then something caught my eye.

I leaned forward. There it was again: a tiny flash of light among the foliage across the river. I stared into the darkness. What the hell was it? A flashlight? No. Something was reflecting the lights on the bridge.

What the hell?

And then I got it. It was either a pair of binoculars and we were being watched... or it was a scope. I jumped to my feet, grabbed Amanda's wrist, and flung her across the room and onto the floor; the tumbler flew out of her hand, upward, hit the ceiling and smashed, showering the room with wine and shards of glass. No sooner did she hit the floor than there was an almighty BANG, and a small hole appeared in the center of the floor-to-ceiling window pane; it fractured, and a spider web of cracks shot out to the edges. It was followed an instant later by a second BANG and another hole appeared; and then, almost in slow motion, the glass wall shattered, came apart and fell inward.

BAM, BAM, BAM. Three more shots rang out on the far side of the river; the bullets slammed into the wall behind me.

It's funny what strange thoughts go through your

head at moments like that. Well, not funny—you know what I mean. My only thought as I crouched down on my knees and the slugs howled over my head was, I hope to hell the neighbors are out.

The shooting stopped, but we stayed down. We were both in the kitchen area, out of sight. I crawled over to the dining table, reached up, grabbed my phone, and punched in 911. Then I looked around at Amanda.

Oh shit.

She was lying on her face on the carpet, her hands to her cheeks, legs spread.

Oh shit, oh shit.

I dropped the phone and crawled over to her. I grabbed her arm and tried to turn her over.

"*Is it over?*" It was more a scream than a shout, but hell, it was music to me. I grabbed her, pulled her to me, and clamped her to my chest.

"Lemme go, dammit! I can't breathe." I heaved a sigh of relief and relaxed my grip; the phone was squawking on the floor. I picked it up and reported shots fired, and gave the dispatcher the address.

"Stay down," I said, releasing her. I crawled over to the side table, grabbed my MP9 out of its holster, chambered a shell, and then crawled over to the window, trying not to put my hands or knees on the broken glass that covered the floor. Impossible.

Cautiously, I peered around the edge of the window frame.

This time I saw the muzzle flash and then, less than a second later, I heard it, BAM. The bullet howled past my face and hit the basement door.

"*Stay down!*" I shouted to Amanda. Then I fired all twelve rounds in my pistol at the spot where I'd seen the muzzle flash. The silence that followed was palpable. The confines of the room had contained the noise of the gunshots, and my ears were ringing. I looked at the nine. The mag was empty, and I didn't have a spare handy. *Damn.*

My fire was not returned, but I wasn't about to get up and show myself. Instead, I sat with my back to the wall and looked around at the train wreck that was now my living room.

I looked over at the couch, and shook my head in awe when I saw the two small holes in the leather. One of them was at the exact spot where Amanda had been sitting. If I hadn't.... Oh my God. It didn't bear thinking about. Once again my instincts, or whatever, had saved a life. This time the life of someone very close to me.

Safely out of sight behind the kitchen wall, I crawled over to her, stood up, and helped her to her feet. She was a mess.

"Here, let me look at you. Turn around."

There were numerous tiny cuts on her bare shoulders from shards of flying glass—none deep, and none that would leave a scar, but that didn't make me feel any better. I shuddered when I thought of what it could have been. I'd almost lost her, and it would have been my fault. I can't describe the overwhelming feelings I had for her at the moment.

Soft? Me? Of course. Aren't we all when it comes right down to it?

I put my arms around her and held her close, her

head on my chest, "Well, sweetheart," I whispered. "This will be a night to remember, that's for sure."

"It's one I want to forget," she whispered back. I couldn't say I blamed her.

"It's over. I think. I need to call Kate."

She answered on the fourth ring. I think she must have been in bed, asleep, because it took a minute for her to grasp what I was saying.

"Stay put," she told me. "I'm on my way."

"Oh, we're not going anywhere." I could hear sirens approaching in the distance. When she arrived fifteen minutes later, the place was already crawling with officers. The beams of a dozen flashlights waved back and forth on the far side of the river. A team of paramedics were attending to the cuts on Amanda's back. Me? I was on my third glass of Laphroaig and feeling no pain.

"Jesus, Harry," Kate said, shaking her head at the offer of a drink. "Who the hell did this?"

"Damned if I know. If I had to guess, I'd say the Archers are behind it. Trouble is, I just can't imagine any one of those three beauties crawling about in the undergrowth over there. Can you? They just aren't the type. If they are behind it, I'd put money on the repo men."

"But surely," Amanda said, shrugging off the paramedic that was trying to take her out to the ambulance, "surely they can't be that stupid. They'd have to know that killing Harry wouldn't stop the investigation." She turned on the medic. "For God's sake, leave me alone, I'm fine." Then she seemed to realize what she'd said. "Oh my God. I'm so sorry. I didn't mean to snap at you. I'll be all right. Thank you for looking after me." He nodded and left her to it. She took a seat at the table next to me.

"True, it would go on," Kate agreed. "If anything it would have stepped it up, several notches. Still...." She rose to her feet, went to the sofa, and fingered the two bullet holes.

"Small caliber," she said, more to herself than anyone else. "Probably a .223 AR15 assault rifle, I shouldn't wonder. Plenty of those in these parts. If we can find one of the slugs we should be able to tell, if they are not smashed all to hell, that is. What are you going to do, Harry? You can't stay here."

"You're right, not until I can get the window repaired and the mess cleaned up. I guess we'll go to Amanda's apartment and stay there for a while."

"That sounds like a plan," Kate said. "In the meantime, I'll have an officer stay here until morning."

"Thanks. I'll call Jacque first thing and have her hunt someone up to either repair the window or board it up. Oh, and you'd better check on the neighbors while you're here, make sure no one was hit by stray bullets."

"That's already been done." She held out her hand and nodded to the MP9 on the table beside me. I sighed and handed it over. I'd get it back sometime next year, I supposed.

I looked at my hands. There were several cuts, one quite deep. One of the medics dug out a chunk of glass and put in a couple of stitches. Afterward I flung some fresh clothes into an overnight bag, grabbed my spare MP9 from the wall safe, took one last look around what was left of my living room, shook my head, took Amanda's arm, and we left.

That night, as we lay together, I couldn't get to sleep. My head was a whirl. Over and over I saw the scope glittering in the darkness, the great window caving inward like a wall of water, Amanda lying face down on the kitchen floor. Time and again I looked at her as she slept. I couldn't help it. I was devastated by thoughts of what might have been, and I was angry.

Someone was going to pay. That was certain.

32

I was still in bed, awake, staring up at the ceiling when my iPhone rang that Tuesday morning. It was Mike Willis.

What the hell? At this time of day?

I looked at Amanda. She was sleeping like a baby. Me? I felt like shit.

"Hey, Mike," I said quietly. "Let me call you back—"

"Wait, wait, we have a match!" he yelled, before I could disconnect. "I got the reports back from the lab, both of them. That tissue with the lipstick you turned in. There was DNA on it. Yours and Ruth Archer's. And Archer's matched the DNA from the hair follicle. You've got yourself a killer."

I felt a surge of excitement, but I also had the strangest feeling, something akin to anticlimax, but more than that. I couldn't explain it, not even to myself. DNA is DNA, and no one can argue with that. Except that.... Well, I had a weird feeling something wasn't quite right.

"I heard you had a bad night," he said. "You got shot at, right?"

"That would be putting it mildly. Look, there are a couple of things I need to sort out and confirm before you turn that information loose. Okay?"

"Well... yeah, but...."

"I know, I know. But I have to sort it through, figure some things out. Tell Kate, of course, but other than that, can you keep it to yourself for a couple of days?"

Silence, and then, "Harry. You know I respect you, right?"

"Of course. Why do you ask?"

"Because you need to know that I wouldn't do what you're asking for anyone else, not even Kate Gazzara. You're asking me to withhold evidence in a murder case. Evidence that I know will put away a killer. I don't know if I can do that, even for you."

"I know, and I understand. I'm not asking you to withhold it. You're going to give it to Kate. Then you'll just sit on it for a couple of days.... One day. You expedited it, right? So it wouldn't have been here for at least that long anyway. One day, Mike. Just one day."

"Oh shit. If this gets out, it'll cost me my job. One day. I'll call Kate now. Don't throw me under the bus, Harry."

"I won't. Count on it. Listen. Do me another favor, please? Give me thirty minutes. I need to call Kate before you do. Deal?"

"Deal."

"Thanks, Mike."

I got out of bed, took the phone into the bathroom, and made the call.

"Hey," Kate said. "How are you? How's Amanda?"

"We're fine. Listen. I just heard from Mike Willis. The DNA reports are in. We have a match—to Ruth Archer. You can expect a call from him in the next few minutes and he'll explain, but here's the thing. I have one of those feelings. I can't put my finger on it. I've asked Mike to give us a little time before he releases the results. I think we need to bring her in, Kate. Right now, but we need to do it without a whole lot of fuss and noise. Just you and me. What do you think?"

She was silent for a minute, then said, "You think it's enough?"

"That's the point. I'm not sure. That's why the need for caution. We don't need to blow it. I'll meet you at Amnicola in say, an hour. Nine thirty. Okay?"

It was.

I went back into the bedroom. The early morning light was shining through the drapes. Amanda was still asleep.

I shook her gently. She rolled over onto her back, looked up me through eyes full of sleep. "What?"

"Hey," I whispered as I pulled her to me. "I missed you."

"Missed me?" she mumbled, still half asleep. "I haven't been anywhere."

"Yes you have. You were asleep, and I missed you."

"Oh, you big baby." She hugged me, then pushed me away, lay back and closed her eyes.

I smiled, got off the bed, and went to the bathroom.

"Coffee please?"

I smiled again. "Yes, ma'am."

I turned on the TV and flipped to Channel Seven. They were talking about the attack, and how their star presenter had been caught up in it.

"How come they haven't called you?" I asked.

"I turned my phone off last night. I suppose I'd better check in. I'm going to ask for a few days off."

I grabbed a quick shower while she was on the phone, dressed—jeans, black T-shirt—climbed into my shoulder rig, slipped my spare MP9 into the holster. I covered it and the holster with a lightweight white golf jacket, and kissed her goodbye. Then I took a deep breath and went down the stairs to my car. Fifteen minutes later I was heading over the Thrasher Bridge at close to seventy miles an hour. I looked at the dash clock. It was almost nine-thirty.

33

Kate was waiting for me when I arrived. Lonnie Guest was with her and, surprise, surprise, he was in plain clothes.

"Hey, Harry," he said, a smirk on his fat face. "I heard they almost got you last night, too bad."

I wasn't quite sure what he meant by that, so I let it go.

"They turned you loose again, huh?" I asked. "Bit early?"

"Yeah, well. The LT couldn't get along without me." He looked at Kate and grinned.

She rolled her eyes. "You ready?" she asked me.

I nodded.

"We'll take a cruiser. Lonnie, you follow us. Stay close."

The fat man was at his desk again when we walked into the offices of the Archer Group. He looked up from his newspaper, started when he saw who it was, rose halfway to his feet, picked up the phone, and punched in a number.

"Starke is here, Ms. Archer, an' he's..." he looked at the badge Kate was holding in front of his nose, "he's got two police officers with him. One is a Lieutenant Gazzara." He listened for a minute then looked up and said, "You can go up."

The door to her office was open. She was seated behind her desk. Her suit jacket was unbuttoned to reveal a semi-transparent white blouse. As always, she looked stunning.

"So," she said. "What do you want this time? Not more bullshit, I hope."

"Ruth Archer," Kate began, holding her badge out for Ruth to see. "My name is Lieutenant Catherine Gazzara. I work in the major crimes unit, homicide division. I need you to come with me to the police department to answer some questions in connection with the death of Angela Hartwell."

"Excuse me," she looked stunned. "Are you insane? What reason could you possibly have? I had nothing to do with her death."

"I have a DNA match that puts you with the body at the time of death."

"That's impossible. She was still alive when I left the club, and I did *leave* the club. I can prove it."

Uh-oh. Here it comes. I thought.

Kate looked at her. "Ms. Archer. We found a hair caught in Angela Hartwell's watchband. It was yours. There's no doubt about it. We have a DNA match. You had to have been there."

"Well I wasn't, lady, and I can prove it. I was with someone, from the minute I left the club until after five the following morning."

"And who might that be?"

She hesitated for a minute, then shook her head and said, in a low voice, "Jack Bentley. It was Jack Bentley. You can ask him. You have it all wrong. I had nothing to do with it."

I didn't look at Kate. I kept my eyes on Ruth. I didn't want her to get the idea we were stumped.

"I still need you to come with me," Kate said. "I'll check your alibi, and if what you say is true.... Well, we'll see. Now, please, if you don't mind...."

She stood. "I need to call my lawyer."

"Of course, and you can do that at the station. Let's go."

We put her in Lonnie's cruiser, and he left with her. We sat together in Kate's cruiser out front of the Archer offices.

"What the hell?" Kate looked at me.

I shrugged. "I guess we'd better go see Bentley, and right now. If not, Drake will have her out before we can get back."

She nodded, started the car, and we headed west.

It was just as Ruth Archer had said. Bentley—very reluctantly—confirmed her alibi. She was with him all night. Unless he helped her, she couldn't have done it. And he didn't, because he stated that he made several cell phone calls from his home that evening, one to say good-night to his wife in Barbados. Those calls could be pinpointed to within a few hundred yards. Ruth Archer was off the hook.

34

"Don't say a word," Kate said to Dan Drake as we walked into the interview room. "You can go," she said to Ruth. "I'll talk to you again if I need to."

Both Drake and Ruth took the easy road and said nothing. They got up and left. Kate and I got coffee from the machine and went to Kate's office.

"Jack Bentley?" she said, dumbfounded. "You've got to be kidding me. Does his wife know, I wonder?"

"I'm sure she does by now. What kind of man screws another woman in his marital bed? Well, with Grace away in Barbados with the girls I guess he wasn't likely to get caught. The cat was away, etc. etc...."

"But what about the hair, the DNA? That was Ruth's. We have a perfect match. Bentley must be lying."

"I don't think so. He didn't want to admit anything. Hell, Kate. We had to twist it out of him. The hair? Planted. Obviously. Yes, the DNA is a match, but If Ruth wasn't there, her hair couldn't have gotten caught in her watch band, and she couldn't have killed Angela, so someone must have planted it." I paused, thinking.

"She couldn't have killed Ralph either," I continued. "The night he died, she was at the club. She was there from four in the afternoon until after ten. I confirmed it with Sol Wise, yesterday evening, when I took Amanda home. I've had him following her for more than a week. That's why I wasn't sure when Mike told me about the DNA match. If she killed Angela, it would have made sense for her to kill Ralph too, especially after the meeting I had with her on Wednesday, right? Anyway, it's a thirty-minute drive from the club to Signal Mountain. She couldn't have done it."

Kate stared at me, her bottom lip between her teeth. "Damn! So if Ruth didn't kill Angela, who the hell did? It couldn't have been Ralph; he was murdered too. And who the hell killed him?"

"Ah, well that's where you're wrong. Ralph could have killed Regis and Angela; he was still alive when she died, remember? If he *did* kill them, the question then becomes who killed Ralph?"

"What about the twins?"

"It's a thought, but I don't think so, because if I'm right, someone went to a lot of trouble to frame Ruth, and that wouldn't have been the twins. It wouldn't make sense. By the same thinking, we can also rule out Burke and Hare."

"So who was it then? And who the hell tried to kill you? Do you have any ideas?"

"I think I do. Think about it."

"I *have* thought about it, you ass. I'm still thinking about it. There's no one else."

"Then think about it some more. Come on, Kate. When all else fails, go back to the basics. Who else besides Ruth would benefit from the deaths of Regis, Angela *and...* Ralph?"

She put her cup down on the desk, threw back her head, and stared up at ceiling, exasperated. *"Regis? Angela? Ralph?* I don't know, dammit...." And then the light went on. "Ohhhhh. I see." She jumped up from her seat, ran round the table, grabbed my cheeks, one in each hand, and shook, hard.

"Ouch," I yelled when she let go. "You got it, then?"

"I got it. Mary Hartwell," she said, triumphantly.

"Yup. Mary. How the hell I missed it before, I don't know. I guess I got fixated on Ruth—okay, okay, not that kind of fixated—and just didn't look for alternatives. It was only when I knew she was out of it, when we were in the car driving here, that I started thinking, and there it was, right in front of us all the time. Everything that benefited Ralph and Ruth also benefitted Mary. Ralph's death benefitted her even more. She now inherits every-thing—at least I assume she does—the Hartwell banks, Angela's money; she gets it all. If Ralph was about to cave, lose his head and try to cut himself a deal... well, she couldn't have that, now could she?"

"Okay, I'll buy in. How do we prove it?"

"That's the $64,000 question, and the answer is... I don't know. Not yet."

She was serious now. "We have nothing. Not a damn

thing. Just a theory. Hell, Harry, it might just as easily have been someone else."

"It might, but it wasn't. She hated Angela. We know that. Regis too. And who else had motive, means, and opportunity to kill Ralph? No one! The only thing we might have is that spot on the rug: the saliva in the blood spatter, and that's real iffy. It might be contaminated, might not even be a match, and we won't even know one way or the other until we get the lab results. And we won't have them for a couple more weeks, at best. If it's not a match, we're fu—Well, you know. Short of screwing a confession out of her, and I can't see that happening, we'll have to begin all over again, at the beginning."

"Oh my God. Chief Johnston will love that. So what do we do?"

"Right now, I'm going to get another cup of coffee. You want one?"

She sighed. "Yeah, black. No sugar."

I went to get it. When I returned, she was sitting forward in her seat staring at a spot on the wall, hands clasped together in front of her, elbows on the desk. She sat up. I handed her the cup. She raised it to her lips and sipped, then looked up at me expectantly.

"Don't look at me like that," I said. "I can't conjure physical evidence out of thin air and, as they like to say around here, we don't got none."

"Come on, Harry; that's not like you. This is what you do. This is why you're a PI and not a cop. You make your own rules. You're a tricky son of a bitch. Think of something."

"What are you saying? That I should go water board her?"

"Something like that." She was smiling when she said it, but there was a wicked gleam in her eye.

I thought about it. Maybe she was right. She *was* right about one thing: I sure as hell didn't have to conform to PD rules and regulations. I sat back in my chair, staring at her, my cup of coffee cradled in both hands. She stared back; her gaze unwavering. For several minutes we stayed like that. Finally, she broke.

"So? What do you think?"

"I think maybe you're right. I should confront her. You can't do it. You can't even be there. If it goes wrong, you'll lose your job. Me, on the other hand.... Dan Drake will come down on me like an avenging angel. I'll get my ass sued off and lose everything I own."

"So you'll do it then?" Her eyes were bright.

I sighed. "You just don't care about me anymore, do you?"

"Of course I do. I just care about snagging Mary Hartwell more." She grinned, showed me those beautiful teeth, and it worked.

"Okay. I'll do it; I'll confront her. If I get it right, we'll have her. If I get it wrong, well... hopefully, I won't. This is what I propose...."

35

The drive up Signal Mountain was pleasant, even though my head was full of mush. The sky was clear and blue, the views spectacular, my mood gleefully vicious. I was heading into the fray, and that's what I live for.

I turned into the driveway, parked, flipped my iPhone onto silent mode, slipped it into my jacket pocket. Then I got out of the car, walked up the steps, and thumbed the doorbell.

She opened the door. "What the hell do you want?"

I blinked. The change from the woman I'd met the day before was startling. Obviously, Mary Hartwell hadn't been expecting visitors. She was wearing black, form-fitting yoga pants and an oversize gray T-shirt. Her hair was a mess.

"I have a few questions, if you don't mind. Can I come in?"

She looked at me, quizzically. "Questions about what?"

"Ralph, of course. What else?"

S he opened the door wider and stood aside for me to pass. I waited while she closed the door, then followed her into the living room.

"Please." She indicated for me to sit in one of a pair of easy chairs. She took the other.

"So. Here you are. What's on your mind, Mr. Starke?"

I looked her in the eye and said, "I know, Mrs. Hartwell. I know everything. I know you and Ralph killed Regis and Angela Hartwell, and I know you killed your husband."

She didn't blink. Her lips were still smiling, but her eyes were not.

"Are you expecting me to take all of that seriously?"

"I am, and I can prove it." The muscles in her neck tightened.

"You're crazy. That's insane." She said it quietly, but without conviction.

"No. Not at all. Let's start with your husband, shall we? That was the easy one, right. He was watching television. You simply walked up behind him and shot him, and then you tried to make it look like suicide." She listened, her face expressionless.

"It's funny how people like you think it's so easy to stage a suicide. It is, in fact, extremely difficult. First, there's gunshot residue to consider. There was none on Ralph's hand. Then there's the blowback, blood spatter; no one ever thinks about that. When a large caliber bullet, or even a small one, is fired into the head at close range, the impact is explosive. Blood and pulverized brain matter are thrown back out of the wound with great force, as you found out, right?"

She didn't answer.

"The blood spatter in this case was extensive," I said. It was all over his shoulder, the chair, the carpet—it even made it into the palm of his hand. Not much. Just a couple of spots, but that was enough. When you put the gun into his hand, those two spots transferred from his palm onto the grip, which means that he could not possibly have shot himself. If he had, his hand would have shielded the grip from the blood spatter."

Again, she gave no reaction.

"But there's more, isn't there, Mary?" I asked.

Now, finally, she shook her head, "I don't know what you're talking about."

"Sure you do. You were covered in it, weren't you? His blood. It was on your face, your clothes, and you must have had your mouth open when you pulled the trigger, because some of the spatter went inside—nasty—and you spat it out. We found it, Mary. Ralph's blood and brain matter... mixed with your saliva. Your DNA."

I'd hit a nerve. Her face was white, her lips drawn tight.

I had her.

And then she shoved her hand down between the seat cushions, brought forth a very large semi-automatic pistol, and pointed it at me. "I may not know much about ballistics, Mr. Starke, but I do know how to use a gun.

The safety is off and there's one in the chamber, so don't try anything."

"Put the gun down, Mary. It's way too big for you, and we both know you'll never get away with killing me."

"Perhaps not, you smug son of a bitch, but I'll have the satisfaction of knowing I beat you. I tried already, you know. That was me on the other side of the river. How's Amanda? I hope the bitch dies."

"Huh. I had that figured for someone else." I paused for a couple of seconds and then said, "You're not going to let me walk out of here, are you?"

She shook her head, smiling.

"Fine," I said, trying to sound unconcerned. *Shit. The bitch is unhinged. I need to play for time.*

"You want to tell me about it?"

"Let's just say I got in over my head and leave it at that."

"Oh come on, Mary. What have you got to lose? Okay then. How about I tell you?" No answer.

"Regis was about to expose Ralph and his check fraud scam, so you had to stop him. You couldn't just murder him. That would raise too many questions, questions you didn't trust Ralph to be able to handle. It had to look like he died of natural causes, so you gave him a heart attack. My question is twofold: how did you pull it off, and what did you use? SUX?"

She couldn't resist it. People like her, narcissists, rarely can, and that's what I'd been banking on.

"SUX?" she asked. "I have no idea what that is. I googled it, of course: How to induce a heart attack. How does anyone do anything these days? I used potassium chloride. It's easy enough to get hold of on the street, if you know the right people. Hell, the article even told me how to do it. Ralph and I went to talk to him. Ralph thought we were going to tell him we would accept his tight-assed offer. Ralph might have been, but I wasn't. Where the hell Angela was, I have no idea; she wasn't home. I slipped a ruffie into his drink, waited until he was out of it, then injected the goo into that big old vein that runs over the ankle bone. All I had to do was pull his sock down. Ten seconds and it was done. He went out like a light. Thirty seconds later, he was dead. I thought Ralph was going to join him, have a heart attack himself. He'd had no clue what I'd been planning. He just stood there like a goddam dopy donkey, and watched. He didn't even ask what I was doing, the dumbass."

Well, I'd asked for it, and she was certainly delivering.

"What about Angela?" I asked.

"That was a little more difficult. It almost got away from me. You're right. She was going to the police with her 'evidence,' as she called it. Ralph bought her a drink at the bar. It was easy enough to slip a ruffie into it. We talked for ten minutes or so. Ralph tried desperately to talk her out of it, but she wouldn't have it. Finally, Ralph gave it up, made some excuse to use the restroom in the lobby, and went out to wait for her. All I had to do was keep her talking for a few minutes more, and I did...." She paused, looked thoughtful, then said, seemingly to herself, "She was a bitch."

She shook her head, as if to rid herself of some unwanted thought, and then continued. "She was already unsteady on her feet when she left. When Ruth grabbed her in the lobby, I thought I was going to lose her, but I didn't. I followed her out. Ralph already was with her, holding her up. We couldn't risk being seen putting her into the car, so we walked her across the golf course to the river. I had to use the flashlight app on my iPhone, it was so dark. By the time we got there, she was completely out of it. I just had to finish it. It was easy enough. Something I'd learned in self-defense class years ago. But I couldn't see in the dark that the water was shallow at that particular spot. I thought the river would take her away."

"CSI found a hair in her watch band," I said. "It was Ruth's. You put it there, right?"

She looked thoughtfully at me. I had a feeling something else was going on in her head, but she continued.

"The hair? Oh.... Yes. That was easy. Ralph was having an affair with Ruth. I'd known about it for months. He knew I knew, and he didn't care. The fool was living in some kind of fantasy world. All she wanted him for were those checks. Anyway, I found the hair on the back of his jacket after one of his nights out. Actually, I found several, and I kept them all in a plastic baggie. Turned out I needed only one. I hooked it into the watch band and... well, as they say: the rest is history. I took her phone and keys. I tossed her phone out of the car window when we crossed the Veteran's Bridge on the way to her apartment. I was hoping we'd find her so-called proof, but we didn't."

"Okay, I can understand all that, but why Ralph? What made you decide to kill him?"

"Ralph was a stupid, weak little man. He'd been chattering on for days after what happened to Angela. When you came around asking questions, he panicked. He was sure you'd figure it out. The damned fool wanted to make a run for it. Hah. For once in his insignificant little life, he was right. You did. Anyway, the idiot was talking about going to Bahrain. Apparently there's no extradition treaty there. He figured he could wire all of the money there and we could live happily ever after." She shook her head at the thought. "He actually thought I would go along with it; spend my days out there baking in the desert. Well, I wouldn't. I hated the little bastard. So I didn't have a choice, did I?"

Something squawked in my jacket pocket. I held up both hands and said, "That's my phone. I should take it. Do you mind?"

She just stared at me, the gun unwavering. I slowly lowered my right hand toward my jacket pocket. The gun moved upward and toward me ever so slightly.

"Easy, Mary," I said. "It's just my phone." I took it slowly from my pocket and, my eyes locked on hers, put it my ear.

"You get all that?" I asked Kate.

"*You bastard!*" Mary shouted, as the door opened.

I started forward. I thought she was going to shoot me. She didn't. Instead she turned the gun upward, stuck the muzzle in her mouth, and pulled the trigger.

BAM.

The impact of the explosion and the heavy .45-caliber bullet flung her backward; the gun flew out of her hand, up and over my head; her chair tipped, and she rolled sideways out of it onto the floor. There was blood everywhere. I thought my eardrums had burst. I didn't hear the police officers rush in. I saw them, but it would be some ten minutes later before my hearing began to return. I looked up. Kate had her hand on my shoulder, mouthing something I couldn't understand. I shook my head, and she grabbed my elbow. I stood. She steered me outside. There were four cruisers already there, and I didn't doubt there were more on the way. I sat in Kate's unmarked and waited. Slowly, my hearing began to return, and I was treated to the cacophony of the sirens of a half-dozen more cruisers, two ambulances—why in God's name did they need two ambulances *and* a fire truck?

The last to arrive was the inimitable Doc Sheddon, ME.

"Hey, Harry," he said as he shambled by toward the open door. "How's it hanging?"

I couldn't help it. Bad as the situation was, I had to smile. The man never changes; nothing ever fazes him.

It's a good way to be, I suppose.

36

It had been two weeks since Mary Hartwell killed herself. The noise from the press had finally died down, though once again I came off as the notorious, hard-ass private investigator. It was starting to get old. A reporter for the Express had managed to get past the police line and snapped a photo of me coming out of the house covered in blood and brains. It was just what they needed. The image had run in the local press and on all of the TV channels for days; it got a mention on CNN and an even bigger one on Fox. Fifteen minutes of fame. I wish that's all I'd ever managed to glean.

It was no wonder then that I received a phone call from Senator Michaels. I think it was more as a courtesy than out of concern. If it took a suicide to stir up some interest, I wondered if it was worth staying in touch with her at all. Ah, maybe I expect too much. Who knows?

The Archers? I bet you're wondering who it was that opened all of those bank accounts. The twins, of course— both of them. They were smart, but not smart enough.

The photo recognition software confirmed that it was one or both of them in the images, but that's not good enough for the courts—reasonable doubt, right? You can't just pick one and go with it; you have to identify the correct one. The records are filled with cases where one twin committed a crime, but couldn't be brought to trial because it was impossible to prove which twin actually did the deed. Our two were betting we couldn't either.

Well, they lost the bet. We could. The images told us the sisters had opened the accounts, and handwriting told us which twin opened which accounts. The FBI compared the applications with known samples of each sister's handwriting and was able to tie each specific account to a particular sister. Cool, huh? I have a feeling the ladies, all three of them, will soon be on vacation, courtesy of the Federal Justice Department.

Speaking of vacations. As soon as I was turned loose after the Mary Hartwell incident, I felt like I needed to get away for a while, that it was time for break.

So I'd taken one—and so did Amanda, milking her compassionate leave for all it was worth. We headed for the hills, to my cabin in the forests of northwest Georgia. It's quiet up there. Peaceful.

Now we were back in Chattanooga, and I didn't feel a whole lot better. Not about my life in general, nor the pain and suffering that seemed to follow me wherever I went in particular. Maybe it was time for me to retire, play a little golf, maybe even write a book. I could afford it.

Nah.

So there we were, on a warm summer evening early

in July. Amanda and I had just enjoyed a quiet dinner and were taking it easy at my place on Lakeshore Lane.

"I don't know if I'll ever feel the same," Amanda said, laying her head back against my arm. We were on the sofa together—a new one—in front of the big window.

"About what?" I asked.

"About sitting in front of this window. I feel all... exposed. It's kinda creepy."

I knew exactly what she meant, because I'd felt it myself. She was right. It would never be the same.

Mary Hartwell's attack had done more damage than I'd thought. Maybe my love affair with the river was over.

"Maybe it's time to move on," I said. "Find somewhere else."

She sat up, turned to look at me. "Seriously?"

I nodded.

"But you love this place."

"I did, but... I don't think I can get past what happened either. I feel like I'll always be... wary, looking for something that isn't there, wondering when it *will* be there. That's no way to live."

"But where would we go?"

"We?" I smiled at her.

"You don't think for a minute you're going anywhere without me, do you?"

I didn't.

THE END

FINALLY

Thank you.

Checkmate was book 4 in the Harry Starke series. If you haven't already read them, you may also enjoy reading the other Harry Starke novels. They are all stand-alone stories: no cliff hangers. **Here's a little about Harry Starke, Book 5, GONE**

Emily Johnston is GONE. She's been GONE for more than a week. She's also the daughter of Harry Starke's one-time boss and nemesis, Chattanooga Police Chief Wesley Johnston. Harry and Chief Johnston haven't seen eye-to-eye in a long time, but when Johnston needs help, he knows there's only one man he can turn to.

But Johnston's jurisdiction ends at the city limits and when Emily's body is discovered in a remote part of the county, Harry has to deal with the imperious sheriff, Israel Hands and two incompetent county detectives. So begins an investigation that will take Harry on a wild ride across Signal Mountain, a case that will include a second murder, two cold cases, sex, alternative lifestyles, and deadly danger for Harry and his friends, until... well, as always, there's a twist in the tale.

To get your copy of **Gone**, CLICK HERE!

If you're a Kindle Unlimited member, you can read GONE for free.

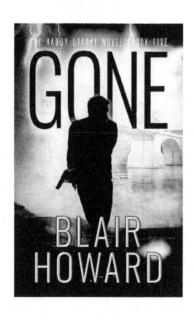